LADY HAWK
AND HER
MOUNTAIN MAN
N GRAY

VINCI
BOOKS

By N Gray

www.ngraybooks.com

Vinci Books

vinci-books.com

Published by Vinci Books Ltd in 2026

1

Chapter One

JANE

I watched from my perch. My enclosure large enough in case I shifted into my human form. But since my capture six weeks ago, I hadn't changed. Not for them. Ever.

It was dangerous staying in my animal form, but it was a risk I was willing to take. I'd rather face those risks than face the dangers that lie ahead.

With my captors fast asleep, they were awaiting their next orders or for morning, whichever came first.

A mouse scurried across the floor, found crumbs dropped when my captors ate, and disappeared into a hole in the wall.

My mouth salivated. It had been too long since I'd eaten —not by choice. The mouse looked tasty. I wanted to nibble on its soft meat. Better yet, I'd love to bite into my captors' soft bellies. They had more meat around their middle and I'd be killing two captors with one satisfactory stone.

Captor One snored, his enormous belly rising and falling as he dreamed of something. He was the strongest of the two, big and burley. He was all muscle, hardly any brain. Well, that's what I thought, anyway.

Captor Two was a skinny man with enough meat to keep me full for a few days. He was the weakest of the two, but a great archer. He hit his target every single time. Ever since I'd been here, I watched him practice on the target across the room, and he never missed. If he ever aimed at me, his arrow would strike. And I didn't need him to threaten me either, because I knew he would aim true.

The lights flickered on, momentarily blinding me. I screeched. The room painfully bright, I cowered in my darkest corner.

The captors awoke with a jolt.

Captor Two raised his bow and pointed his arrow at me. Even in a dreamy state, his reflexes were sharp and trained on me.

Their leader, Rhett, entered the room. He held his head up high, combed his fingers through his dark hair, and his black eyes shimmered with knowledge. I didn't like this look. He was cruel, and I imagined what he'd do next. Whatever he planned never ended well for me.

Trailing behind Rhett was my Michael—my protector. His body bruised and broken. His torn clothing caked with blood. Blood he'd spilled for me. Blood he'd gladly give to protect me. It broke my heart watching him suffer. I wanted to give in to Rhett's demands, but Michael had said, 'no'. I needed to stay in my hawk form and never give in to Rhett's demands, no matter what he did to Michael.

"Jane, I'm glad to see you're still awake. It would be much simpler if you just changed," Rhett groaned, emphasizing the word 'changed'. He reached for the clothing I'd first worn, bringing it towards his nose, and breathed deeply.

I shuddered and squawked, flapped my wings as I

showed my disapproval. Some of my feathers floated around me like snow flurries.

The evening was cool and I suspected winter was near. I needed all my feathers to stay warm.

"Change for me Jane. If you care about Michael. Do it!" Rhett growled, his glassy black eyes boring holes into me. I shivered at the thought. I knew what he was capable of. As hard as it was for me not to give in, I couldn't or Michael's torture would be for nothing.

Rhett harrumphed. "Michael doesn't have much longer, my dear. Do you want him dead?" Rhett raised his hand, pointed two fingers at Michael, and slashed his fingers in the air like knives. Two slashes formed on Michael's broad naked chest, followed by blood.

I squawked again.

"Don't do it, Jane," Michael mumbled. His lips swollen and cracked. The skin around his eyes finally healing and could see me. His blue eyes filled with sadness and with little strength he had left. I didn't know how much longer he had to live, but he was suffering. Every day since our capture, Rhett had tortured him. Slowly, Michael was dying because of me.

Rhett approached the cage with long tweezers, reached inside, and removed one of my golden feathers. My feathers no longer as golden, but a faded yellow. He placed the feather into a contraption to measure the gold content. It flashed red.

Rhett shook his head. "You're weakening, Jane. If I can't get what I need for the elixir, you're messing with my entire production line. Do you understand the consequences?" he said gravely.

I kept quiet, staring at him with my beady black eyes through the bars.

"Your kind will die with you if you don't do what I ask. I'm here to help you—"

"No, you're not. All you want is her precious feathers," Michael spluttered, blood dripping out of his mouth while his chest wound continued pumping blood. They weren't helping him. They weren't seeing to his wounds. They were leaving him to die like a wild animal.

I turned my focus on Rhett and wanted to pick at his soft eyeballs. They would be a tasty treat I'd savor and remember for the rest of my life.

"That's where you're wrong, *protector*. I want to ensure her kind lives on. I will breed with her, create more little hawks and watch them flourish. And if their gold is as pure as their mothers, then we'll all be happy for it. It's a win-win situation," Rhett grinned. His dark eyes flashed with murky oil. He was evil to the core.

I didn't know what flavor evil Rhett was, I only sensed he was one of the worst. Rhett didn't shift into any creature, nor did he drink blood. But there was something about him I sensed was pure evil. It was possible he was the devil's spawn—created to unleash his wicked deeds.

"It's time to decide, Jane," Rhett continued, pacing in front of my cage. "Michael won't last much longer." Rhett raised the same hand, slicing his fingers through the air once more.

I screeched.

Michael collapsed to his knees, gripping his neck to stop the bleeding, but his life essence pulsed between his fingers; his carotid artery shredded.

"Don't give in to him, Jane," Michael said in a hoarse voice. "Don't. I signed up to protect you now and forever. Allow me to die with honor."

Rhett laughed as he left. "One more day, Jane," he sang as he disappeared out the room.

The two men who held Michael left him where he'd fallen and disappeared with Rhett.

My two captors did nothing but stare at Michael as he bled.

Michael crawled on weak limbs towards the cage. Ignoring his deep wounds, he still only cared for me, wanting to protect me.

My heart broke. More feathers fell. I flapped my wings, desperately needing to get out. I needed to save my Michael. He was dying because of me.

"Don't give in to him, Jane," Michael whispered, his face near the bars. "Get out of here. Once you're out, get your strength back. Understand that Rhett will never stop coming after you. You need to kill him. I know you can. Do it. Don't let this be in vain," Michael said weakly as he glanced at the captors, then turned back to me. "Grab my bracelet and fly away, Jane. Don't come back to save me. Nothing can save me now, but you can save yourself," Michael said softly, pulling a key from his back pocket and silently unlocked my cage.

Somehow he'd gotten the key—it was a risky move, but I appreciated it.

Slowly, Michael stood with the last of his energy; his legs shaky as more blood flowed down his body. As he yanked the door open, he lunged at my captors before they could react.

"Fly, Jane!" Michael yelled as a blade flashed in the air, striking Michael's chest.

I flapped my wings, was out of my cage, and grabbed the golden bracelet from the hook on the wall. When I'd secured the bracelet in my beak, I flew to the window. The window wide enough for me to squeeze through, and then I was out.

I couldn't turn back to see if Michael was okay. I knew he wouldn't be, not after seeing Captor One stab him. If I went back, it would be the end of me. They'd put me back inside my cage until I withered away.

I caught a wind pocket, flapped my large wings with all the energy I had left, and flew as hard and as fast as I could. But I was weak. My body was hurting, all the while mourning the loss of Michael. But I couldn't give up now. I had to do what Michael said; leave, get healthy, and find my way back.

Captor Two yelled out the window.

I didn't look behind; I needed to get far away quickly.

Something thwished, then whooshed past me. An arrow missed my right wing. Then the air changed as another arrow zipped past, closer this time.

All I focused on was getting away. I pushed my tortured body to fly harder and faster. I could never survive another round of torture, nor would I give Rhett the satisfaction.

Before I soared higher, another arrow thwished through the air, but this time it didn't go past. It struck my wing.

Chapter Two

BYRON

The axe cut through the log with ease, splitting it into two manageable sizes for firewood. A motorized sound caught my attention. I dropped the axe, picked up my shirt, and wiped my brow. I spied my Glock near my water bottle and stepped closer in case I needed it.

In the distance I saw dust. Then the vehicle slowly came into focus. It was just Paul, the local grocery store owner. He pulled up in his large all-terrain vehicle and killed the engine. For a large, imposing man he was awfully friendly even with dark eyes, unbrushed brown hair and a bushy beard. He reminded me of a grizzly bear with a heart of gold, but just as deadly.

He grunted as he climbed off his ATV and approached. "Christ, the older I get, the harder it is getting off these things," he mumbled, dusting his jeans.

I chuckled lightheartedly, watching this burly man dismount from his ATV.

"I got your message," he said with one outstretched hand to shake mine.

"You didn't have to reply in person," I said with humor and slapped his back while we did that sideways manly hug.

"I'm on my way to the store, anyway," he said, surveying the area. Coming here was completely out of his way, but I appreciated the effort. He glanced from my head to my toes with a faint smile on his face. "I'm waiting for my delivery before I can deliver yours. I'll get one of my guys to bring your food parcel tomorrow, maybe throw in a candy bar. You're looking thin."

"I'm fine. You know how it is out here. Besides, the last thing I need is a trip to the dentist." Although I was running low on food, I was going hunting this afternoon, anyway. I'd just cut enough meat to last the week.

"Anyway, I guess I'll be off then," Paul said, stepping backwards. If I didn't know any better, I'd say he hesitated.

"I'll let you know if I need anything else." I moved with him. "Don't look so worried."

"You know I don't like you living out here on your own."

"I'm a big boy—"

"I know you can handle yourself," he said with an undercurrent of concern. "Anything can happen out here. And if you're alone, it's only that much harder."

"I'm fine, really. Thanks for checking in on me."

Paul checked up on me once a month, but this was his second time already. I slapped his back as he mounted his ATV and sat there, staring at me. Paul and I went way back and knew what each could handle. But him staring at me like that left me concerned, even though there was nothing for him to worry about.

"The wife wants you over for dinner next week. Can you make it?"

"I'll see what I can do."

Paul smiled, knowing I would make an excuse not to go. Their house was about a three-hour hike back towards town. I'd been there a few times since I'd moved here, but had declined the last couple of invites. They owned property that bordered on the outskirts of Sterling Meadow and the forest. They, like me, preferred nature to humans, but they still needed some human contact—I didn't.

I watched Paul leave. He didn't turn around like he always did. Then he disappeared.

I chopped the rest of the firewood and packed them near the cabin. Once the area was clean, I readied myself for the hunt.

It's dark. The only sounds came from insects; they kept me company with their stridulating music. They kept my mind focused and in the zone.

There's a slight breeze from the South. The temperature had dropped three degrees since I'd been out here. But nothing could stop me from getting my target.

Movement in the shadows caught my eye. I pointed my rifle in that direction and peered through the scope; a deer in my crosshairs.

My stomach rumbled. Paul was right. I hadn't eaten in two days and had to eat tonight. I'd placed my monthly order a little late this month and suffered the consequences. It was my fault. I used to have a standing order, which I changed since I didn't always get through some of the tinned food. I had rice left, but it wasn't the same as protein.

A chill swept through me. The cold, moist air could hamper my shot. But I'd used my rifle in worse temperatures before. I could make the shot easy.

I pressed my finger gently on the trigger, the connection automatic, almost sacred.

The deer moved from behind the tree and in the kill shot. I didn't hesitate. I exhaled and pulled the trigger, maintaining my position. The deer fell with a satisfactory thump.

My clothing stuck to my skin. My heart rate slowing as I kept watch through the scope for any other movement. There was none. No matter how many times I did it, I still felt the aftereffects; the adrenaline dump, then the shakes.

I pocketed the shell casing and picked up my weapon. The surrounding forest deadly quiet, not even the crickets were active. The deer lay where I'd dropped her; one shot to the head. She didn't suffer. She didn't know what hit her. It calmed me to know I hadn't hurt her. I only hunted to eat. I didn't kill on purpose anymore.

I placed my rifle on the ground, unsheathed my hunting knife, and only took what I needed. I said a prayer once I'd packed my meat into packaging and into my backpack. The wild cats, mountain lions, or even the wolves would eat the rest. I wasted nothing, as nature had intended.

The hike back to my cabin took longer. The wind had picked up and rain had fallen.

I preferred not to hunt where I slept—I didn't want any predator near my home apart from me. I didn't want to kill unnecessarily.

After they'd discharged me, I cashed in what money I had, bought a piece of land near water in the mountains, and built my home. A one bedroom cabin with everything I needed. It was enough for me to live comfortably and off the earth.

The tranquility of my home kept me here. I didn't mind going into the nearby town, Sterling Meadow. I just preferred to live away from others. I already had my fill of evil beings and the company they kept. And I'd destroyed enough lives to last me ten lifetimes. The less I saw of others, the better for my sanity. I chose to live out here with nobody around except me and nature.

My nights were quiet with no man-made sounds; cars, trucks, digging or other. It was only me, the quiet of nature, and the soothing animal and insect sounds.

By the time I reached my cabin, the weather had worsened, and it was dark. I went around back to start the generator. I switched on a light and dropped my backpack on the kitchen counter. The wind continued beating against the walls and roof—a cacophony of sounds echoing within the walls.

Before doing anything else I checked the laundry, bedroom and bathroom—all was as I had left it. The cabin smelled of gun oil, wood, and hints of coffee with my mug still on the kitchen counter from this morning.

Once content nobody had entered my place, I cleaned fat off the meat and chopped it into smaller portions. I bagged the steaks and placed them in the deep freeze.

I rounded my shoulders; pain laced down my right-hand side. My body aching from holding the same position for hours. A massage would be great, but only one thing helped.

Outside my cabin, I had a natural hot spring. That's one reason I chose this spot—for that hot spring. It comprised a whole heap of natural minerals which didn't hurt.

I exited my cabin and stripped naked. The chill of the wind caressed my skin. I brushed sand and dried blood from my ankles. I hadn't realized I'd hurt myself until I saw the gash above my ankle bone. Luckily, I didn't need stitches.

I climbed into the hot rocky pool; the contradicting

sensations from my chilled body in the hot spring knocked my breath away. But I instantly felt better and relaxed in the heated water.

The rock pool was small enough for three adults to sit comfortably. You couldn't dive in or you'd break your neck. But deep enough to stand in, reaching my chest.

Surrounding the pool were natural jets that filled the hot spring with scalding water, which cooled as it reached the surface.

I sunk below the surface to wet my face and hair. My feet touching the bottom rocks with grassy patches in between. The heat from the natural jets struck my aching muscles in my back, and I instantly relaxed against the rocky sides and glanced up at the sky. The tension building slowly seeping away as the wound on my ankle itched and I exhaled slowly.

After about twenty minutes, the weather threatened to blow me away. I climbed out, dried with a towel I'd kept outside, and already the wound on my ankle had healed—leaving behind a thin scab.

I wondered what was inside the water that gave it the healing properties, but I'd never question it. It was a blessing I'd gladly accept. It amazed me nobody had found it before I stumbled upon it.

One day I went hiking in search of land to call home and I literally fell into it. A thin layer of moss had covered the surface of the hot spring and I was so focussed on my surroundings I hadn't noticed the water until I fell into it. Then when I noticed my aching joints easing, I enquired about purchasing this land, and the government accepted my offer. Even after investigating the hot springs' origins, I'd found out nobody knew of its existence. I didn't tell Paul about it in case word got out, and he was my friend. I thought of it as something for me to protect. Should others find out about it, they may destroy it.

Once dressed I fried a steak and ate. Then I enjoyed a cup of tea on my porch. All the cabin lights were off. The pond and the forest beyond my front yard all bathed in moonlight. The pond water rippled with silver light was therapeutic to witness, with the stars bursting with their brilliance.

I sat peacefully in my chair, listening to the howling wind and watching the soft rain seep into the ground. The heaviness of the day fading as the chamomile tea and surroundings calmed me.

The sounds of a nearby hooting owl caught my attention. Stridulating crickets sounded behind my cabin. And leaves crunched underfoot as animals walked past. These were the sounds I wanted to hear.

The smell of rain filled the air as I breathed in through my nose, with dampness clinging to my jacket. I suspected a storm approaching from the north, and would feel the force of it by tomorrow.

My hackles raised the moment a stillness filled the space. I didn't hear what had caused it, but I sensed *something*. Not sure what it was, but I needed to investigate.

I placed my mug on the floor beside my chair and reached for the secret compartment at my feet, unsheathed a hunting knife, and grabbed my Glock with the silencer. I closed the lid on the compartment and stood up.

My porch had a few creaks, so instead of using the stairs I jumped over the railing onto soft ground, muffling my landing.

Somewhere behind my cabin I heard a sound; muffled cries of an animal.

Gentle rain sprinkled on my shoulders. The ground

damp with puddles. In a crouched position, I ran around my cabin, sticking to the shadows. My eyesight was good but I couldn't see far without my night goggles; I'd placed them in another compartment in the cabin, but out of reach. I would make do with what I had and continued in the sound's direction.

Another hunter, perhaps?

I'd encountered two hunters since living here. They were friendly. But I learned never to trust anyone. There could be a child with a doll in one hand and a grenade in the other. I trusted nobody.

Squinting up ahead, a shadow moved, stumbling. It was an injured animal or someone trying to ambush me.

I approached quietly, blending with the surrounding darkness.

Whimpering sounds came from that direction. Someone crying. The sounds were mournful and filled with pain.

I lowered my weapon but kept it ready with my knife firmly in my left hand—ready to slice and dice if I needed to.

The person tried to stand but kept falling, reminding me of a toddler trying to walk. I furrowed my brows as I neared. Not believing what I was seeing, I edged on closer without them noticing me.

If I didn't know any better, I'd assume it was a boy; short hair, slim body. But when I saw her naked breasts, I knew something was wrong. This was a trap. No woman stood naked in the middle of the forest. And to watch her unable to walk screamed suspicious—this was one trap I wouldn't fall for.

Why was she here?

She could be a witch needing body parts. A shifter

trying to change. A vampire needing blood. Or something else.

I needed to understand what she was and why she's here —and alone. I waited five minutes for others to join her but nobody did. It was only her battling to stand.

Her cries continued. Her left arm kept going to her right shoulder as she struggled to her feet. Something was wrong. Possibly injured.

I neared, taking a wider girth around her. I sensed nobody else. No footprints in the sand or disturbed bushes. There were no insects here either. And the only sounds came from her.

I approached from the back and cleared my throat.

"Hello? Is someone out there?" she said. Her voice meek and filled with pain. "I need help... hello?"

"What are you doing here?" I asked gravely as I showed myself, aiming my weapon at her head.

She raised her left arm, her right arm limp against her side with an arrow through her shoulder, and blood pouring down her side.

"What happened?" I pointed my weapon at her shoulder, then back at her head.

"Please, I'm hurt and mean you no harm. Can you help me get it out and then I'll be on my way," she cried. A soft whimper escaped her lips when she tried to stand.

"Are your legs injured?"

"No, I... um... please, I need help?"

I glanced around, but there was nobody else out here except us. There was no one about to jump out and kill me, us.

As much as I didn't want to take her inside my cabin, I couldn't leave her out here alone. But finding a naked, injured woman in the forest with nobody else around was irregular. She was trouble and could bring trouble to me.

But if anyone needed help, I was the right person. I could help her, even though I didn't want to. Although I didn't want trouble in my life, I couldn't leave her on her own when I knew I was capable of assisting.

"I don't want trouble," I said, echoing my thoughts.

"I don't mean to bring you any. But if you help me, I'll leave soon after. I promise. I don't want anyone else getting hurt because of me." She wiped her cheeks. She was crying.

Christ, I hated tears. I couldn't leave her out here, even though I didn't understand how she got hurt or how she got here. But she was naked, unarmed, and bleeding.

I sheathed my hunting knife inside my belt near my back and secured my weapon beside it. I needed to carry her, but she was very naked and I didn't know how best to pick her up without either of us feeling uncomfortable. She didn't seem too concerned with her nudity, but it bothered me. I hadn't seen another woman in over a year, never mind a naked one. I exhaled a shaky breath, removed my warm jacket, and handed it to her.

"Thank you," she said and slipped her left arm inside, then only covered her right shoulder in such a way that the protruding arrow didn't ruin my top, but still covered her flesh. She made an *ooh* sound and snuggled into my jacket. "This feels good. It's so, so warm." A smile tugged on her lips and for a moment I felt something… joy.

"Can you stand?" I asked. The uneasiness I'd felt earlier was back now that I actually had to touch her.

She shook her head. "No, I haven't… uh… in a while."

I didn't know what she meant. "I can't treat you out here so I'll need to pick you up." I motioned at her legs. "You're naked." I stated the obvious. "Are you okay if I, uh, touch you under your legs?" I didn't say I might need to touch her ass, but I'd get to that part if I needed to. I just hoped my erection didn't get bigger.

"Uh-huh," she mumbled, and got comfortable, ensuring my jacket remained closed over her breasts and other parts I could no longer see.

I swallowed hard as I stared down at her delicate form, and something tugged in me. Unsure of what that was, and ignored it. I needed to treat her wound and get her on her way again.

The rain continued drizzling, wetting her hair and porcelain skin. She licked her fine lips. My eyes darted to her long legs and feet.

I had to just get this over with, touch her bare legs and press her body against mine as I carried her. It was easy and I could do it. Christ, when visions of her naked body flashed before me again, I swallowed hard. A nervousness swept through me, reminding me of my teenage years.

This was stupid. I was being ridiculous.

Then, in one swift motion, I reached for her. My left arm slipped under her knees. My right hand snaked around her back and under her right arm without touching the arrow.

Christ, she could fit easily in my arms. And that strange tugging sensation happened again.

She was warm against my chest. Her skin soft against my fingertips, and she smelled of flowers; lavender, roses, and something else.

She wrapped a slender left arm around my neck, flinching as she moved her right hand to keep my jacket closed and without moving the arrow too much.

In one swift motion, I lifted her up, her side completely

against my chest and jeans. I hoped my belt buckle wasn't cutting into her flesh.

"Is this okay?" I asked. "Nothing cutting into you?"

"No, I'm fine." She smiled sweetly, although I sensed she was in a lot of pain.

"What's your name?" I asked, keeping the moment light and to get my mind off her naked body against mine. I hoped she couldn't feel my growing erection digging into my jeans.

"Jane," she said, looking me in the eye. The color of her irises was a mixture of grass green with hints of honey-brown. Her nose thin and dainty, her lips thin and parted, and her cheek-bones high. She would be beautiful if not for the emaciated appearance. Starved and bleeding; I didn't know if she would survive the night.

I glanced down at the slender slope of her neck and relieved my jacket covered most of her. But the top part of her breast showed, and I groaned inwardly. *Fuck!* She was beautiful and here I was, pawing her like a wild animal with my large hands.

I didn't know if she felt uncomfortable having a stranger carry her, but I sure felt uncomfortable carrying a half-naked, injured woman.

"I'm Byron," I said, introducing myself and traversed down the path towards my cabin.

I felt like the only person in the world when she smiled at me.

Jane was a lightweight, which added fuel to my suspicion that she was undernourished. With each step she flinched, but didn't cry out. It hurt me to feel her subtle movements without alerting me to the fact that she was in pain, but I saw it on her face. To ease her discomfort, I tried stepping lighter.

Finally, we reached my cabin, and I watched her expression change from hurt to wonder.

"Wow, your place is beautiful," she said. Her eyes glistening in the moonlight.

I traversed up the porch stairs, pulled the door handle down and pushed it open with the side of my body, and eased inside. I felt for the light switch and flicked it on.

"There's only one bedroom, but you can stay there."

"Thank you." She swallowed hard. "I didn't mean to inconvenience you. It should only take a day or two, then I'll leave."

"It's no problem." I settled her on my bed and opened my closet. I handed her a pair of pants, socks, and a t-shirt. "They're big but I suppose it's better than nothing." I tried for humor but it didn't work.

She took the clothing graciously and nodded. "Thank you."

"I'm going to get my medical supplies and remove that arrow." I didn't wait for her reply as I closed the door and fetched my first aid kit.

Chapter Three

JANE

Pain laced the right-hand side of my body. Every time I moved, it felt as if the arrow sliced through my flesh. My blood flowed while I weakened, ruining Byron's jacket and bedding.

I hoped Byron could remove the arrow and stop the bleeding before I bled out.

The moment I'd landed I managed to shift into my human form; it was something I hadn't done in weeks. As shifters, we rarely stayed in our animal form for longer than a day, two at the most. We risked going mad, not able to shift back, or certain death. I was incredibly lucky to have managed the change.

I had to remain a hawk to avoid Rhett's supposed affection—something he had always spoken about, but I doubted the man had it in him to care for anyone but himself.

When the arrow lodged in my shoulder, I knew I needed help, and that meant human help. I needed to shift into my human form, since no human would help a hawk.

It would be easier to kill an injured bird, and I didn't want to risk it.

Apart from the arrow sticking out of my shoulder, my shifting back into human form hurt as my muscles pulled and tendons snapped back in place. My change sucked the last bit of energy, and I crumpled against the tree.

When I felt I had enough energy I tried to stand, but my knees kept buckling. Since I'd been in my hawk form for weeks, my legs were too weak to carry me. And the food Rhett and his captors had given me was not enough to sustain me. The tiny morsels were enough to keep me from passing out. I needed help and was grateful when Byron came along.

But I knew I posed a threat to Byron's safety by being in his home. I was sure once he removed the arrow, and I'd eaten enough, I'd have enough strength to continue. The farther away I got from Byron, the better. Then once I reached the nearest town, I could get lost in the sea of humans. I'd done it before. I could do it again, except the last time Michael had been with me. He had been there to protect me.

I twisted the golden bracelet around my wrist as I thought of Michael. An overwhelming sadness washed over me but I couldn't mourn my him or my people yet. I needed my strength so that I could go back the way I came and find Rhett. I had to avenge my people.

When Byron exited his room and closed the door, I removed his jacket, and slipped on the sweat pants as carefully as I could without hurting my shoulder. The moment I pulled on socks, my body warmed immediately. Unfortunately, I couldn't pull the shirt on all the way. Instead, I slipped the shirt over my head and left arm, but kept my right shoulder out until Byron removed the arrow.

I lay on my left-hand side, facing the wall and door, waiting for Byron's return.

When a knock sounded, I said he could enter.

Byron opened the door slowly, ensuring I was decent, and sat on the floor near me.

"I have morphine injections if you need—"

"No!" I yelled. "Sorry, no, thank you," I said softer. "No pain medication." I didn't need any pain meds. It did nothing for me, anyway. But that didn't mean I could trust Byron not to slip me something so potent it knocked me out. Besides, I needed to shift back into my hawk to heal as soon as the arrow was out.

"Nothing?" he asked, shock laced in his tone.

"No, you can clean the wound with saline, break the tip of the arrow off and pull it through my shoulder." I'd seen it done before, but it never happened to me.

"You realize it's going to hurt with no pain meds."

"It's okay, just do it." I exhaled audibly. "Please."

"Yes, ma'am," Byron said, and got to work. He pulled a pair of bolt cutters out of his bag and cut off the arrowhead. The movement caused the arrow to move sideways, tearing a cry from me.

"Are you okay?"

"Uh-huh," I lied, "please hurry." My vision darkened with bright, sparkly stars as tears slipped down my cheeks.

Byron placed the arrowhead in a metal bowl and hovered over me for a better look at the wound.

The pain eased, and I could focus on my surroundings once more. Byron was so close. I watched his corded muscles bunch as he worked on my shoulder. The smell of cotton detergent wafted in the air that must've come from his clothing. Before I could decipher any other smells, I felt

22

the heat from his body when his large hand touched my shoulder while the other reached for the arrow.

"You ready?" he asked with one hand on the arrow and the other holding onto my shoulder.

I nodded, bracing myself for what's coming.

"One... two..." He didn't get to three. He yanked the arrow out of my back with a slurpy swish sound.

I flinched, then screamed when the full force of pain slammed into me. I bit into my knuckles to shift the pain elsewhere, but it didn't work. My vision tunneled as my world faded. My pulse thundered in my ears. Then I remembered to breathe. I unclenched my jaw from my knuckles and sucked in air. My shoulder throbbed with molten pain, along with lava flowing into my veins.

"It's okay, it's out." He placed the broken arrow in a larger tray and got to work cleaning the wound.

The pain intensified when he added the saline. My shoulder continued to burn with no sign of it letting up.

Byron cleaned with saline, using fresh gauze to wipe the area each time. After about a minute, there was a heap of blood-soaked gauze in the silver bowl, but Byron continued cleaning. Finally, he huffed. I didn't know him well enough to decipher his tones or expressions, but that didn't sound right to me.

"What's wrong?" I asked, wincing while trying to glance over my shoulder. But I couldn't see anything with his arm blocking my view.

"It doesn't want to stop bleeding. And there's a yellow/brown gel in the wound," he said, glancing back at the arrow, then at the wound. He reached for the metal arrowhead and inspected it. "It's laced with something." He brought it near his nose and sniffed. "It's an oily substance and smells rancid." Byron placed the arrow tip back in the metal bowl and stared at me. "What happened, Jane? Who did this to you and why?" He sat back on his haunches, his hands bloody but he didn't seem to care that he'd forgotten to use surgical gloves even though he'd brought a pair to use.

I didn't want to involve him and didn't think he needed to know my life story. Because I wasn't staying here, I could get away with telling him something. But when I looked at his friendly face and kind eyes, I couldn't involve him and thought it best not to say anything.

"Maybe just add gauze, wrap my shoulder tightly, and give me some food. Meat preferably. Then I'll get on my way."

"You can barely walk..." he left his sentence hanging and exhaled a frustrated breath. "Why won't you tell me?"

"Because you've done enough, and I don't want harm coming your way," I snapped back, my tone harsh. "Sorry." I winced and sat up. I'm sure I flashed him my breasts— *again*—but he didn't seem to notice. I was comfortable naked around others, but wasn't sure if he was.

"Don't you think it's a little too late for that. You're in my home, bleeding on my bed and I have your blood on my hands." He raised his hands for emphasis. My blood dripped down to his elbows and onto his pants.

I cringed, exhaling loudly. "They don't know where I am and they don't know *you*." I sat upright and moved my toes; it felt like pins and needles stabbing my feet. Now that my legs were waking up, I should be able to walk soon. I reached for the gauze, but Byron grabbed my hand.

"Fine, at least let me cover the wound," he said when he realized I would say nothing else.

I allowed him to treat the wound even though it continued seeping blood and the strange yellow/brown gel mixed with my blood. I sniffed near the area once bandaged, and it reminded me of a decaying body.

"Yeah, that doesn't smell right, does it? I need to put a drip on you, you've lost a lot of blood."

"No," I shook my head, "no drip, no meds. I need food and then I'll go." I mumbled as I slipped my arm through the sleeve. On shaky legs, I stood up.

Byron climbed to his feet and backed away from me. I took a step forward and my knees buckled.

"You aren't going anywhere, Jane," Byron grumbled as he sat me back down. "Have you always been this stubborn?" He lifted my legs and placed them on the bed.

I laughed sadly, thinking of Michael and what he'd usually say to my stubbornness. Then I thought of his sacrifice and couldn't stop the tears. My chest ached as my heart broke.

"Ah, shit, I hate seeing women cry." Byron exited the room, returning a moment later with a toilet roll. "Here," he handed it to me, "I don't have tissues. And all I have to eat is fresh deer meat."

"I'll have it medium rare please." I took the toilet roll from his hands. "Thanks," I said. My fingers brushed against his and my fingertips tingled. I ignored the sensation, tearing off a few pieces to wipe my face and blow my nose.

"Sure, one medium rare deer steak coming up."

"Can I have two?"

He chuckled lightheartedly. "Sure."

Chapter Four

BYRON

Christ, she was stubborn; I thought as I cleaned the skillet I'd used earlier and placed it on the stove. I switched on the flame to heat the pan, removed a couple of steaks from the fridge and placed them in the hot pan. Then I fried her steaks for a couple of minutes on each side, ensuring they came out medium-rare.

This woman had been through an awful experience and survived. No *human* could survive; Jane was terribly thin, shot with an arrow laced with poison, and she'd lost a lot of blood. Which reminded me I needed to order another mattress and jacket now that she'd ruined both.

What caught me off guard was she didn't want any pain medication, which sent all the hair on my body standing on end.

Jane was not human.

I should be afraid, but I wasn't. I'd seen it all and been through enough to last me ten lifetimes.

She didn't seem like a vampire, besides; they didn't eat

steak. Vampires enjoyed blood directly from the source. She didn't look at my neck once.

Perhaps she was a shifter; which one I didn't know, but I'd ask. The last thing I wanted was her shifting into her beast and attacking me.

I plated the steaks, grabbed cutlery, and entered my room. She'd managed to push herself against the head-board in a seated position. Her bandaged wound red with blood dripping down her arm. The poison stopped her blood from clotting, and if that wasn't rectified soon, I didn't think she'd survive.

"You're still bleeding," I said, handing her the plate.

Jane waved my hand away without responding. Instead, she eyed the steaks, nodding absently as she dug in. She picked up the first steak with her hands and enjoyed a big bite, chewed, then another bite. She hummed as she enjoyed her meal, finishing the first steak quickly, then ate the second one a little slower—savoring it more.

In less than ten minutes, the steaks eaten, and she licked her fingers. I watched her intently as she sucked the juices from her fingers; her eyes no longer sunken into their socket and her cheeks were rosy.

"Which were-animal are you?" I asked, removing the plate from her lap.

She stopped mid-lick, her eyes on me and darkening. And if I didn't know any better, I'd say she scowled.

I raised my free hand in mock-surrender. "I'm only asking. Perhaps I can help you better if I know which were-animal you are. And besides, how do I know you won't go rogue on my ass and chew my head off. I have a book I can browse—"

"I'm not a praying mantis and I won't be in any book."

My eyebrows shot up in surprise. I had every were-animal known in that book. "I'd find that surprising."

"Bring your book here, let me have a look." She challenged.

I placed the plate in the kitchen sink and fetched my book. Every marine received one of these. We had to know our enemy. Of course, it wasn't the shifters who were our enemy. We didn't kill many—only those who had gone rogue, or we had orders directly from the top.

The bookshelf stood against the far wall of the living room. I grabbed the book I needed and entered my room, handing it to her.

She paged through it carefully, one eyebrow raised, no doubt silently judging me. "You killed were's?"

"They trained me to, yeah, but I didn't kill many. Only those who deserved it."

"Are you sure they deserved it?"

"Yes, ma'am. I sat with my spotter for days, watching our targets. Every one of them deserved it. They were all terrible."

"I'm glad to hear. Is that why you live alone in the forest?" She glanced up. Her eyes focused on mine as if she could see directly into my soul; silently judging me, or even hating me without knowing me.

"Let's just say I preferred the comfort of nature."

She gave a curt nod and continued paging through the index, her finger caressing the pages as she searched for her animal. "Huh," she said, "not here."

"I find that hard to believe. Now you must tell me what you are," I said, taking the book from her.

"I'm the last of my kind, Byron," she said with sorrow in her tone, and her eyes glistened in the dim light. She didn't offer any more information as she remained guarded.

I got the sense she felt threatened by everyone she met. Which would explain her hesitance to reveal much. Whichever animal she was, she was being hunted. The poisonous arrow and the wound in her shoulder spoke volumes. Whoever had hurt her wanted her dead.

"I won't hurt you, Jane," I assured her and meant it. She had done nothing to me and no matter what animal she was, I wouldn't hurt her. I did not do senseless killings. Ever. Unless she was a kingpin drug lord selling drugs to five-year-olds. Then I'd take great pleasure in removing her head.

I leaned against the wall, waiting for her answer. She seemed to think about it. Finally she opened her mouth and said, "I'm a hawk."

"A hawk?" My brows furrowed. I'd never heard of a shifter hawk before.

"Uh-huh, a lady hawk."

My smile reached my eyes as I imagined her as this large, majestic creature. Then my smile fell flat. "Why are you the last of your kind? And why are they trying to kill you?" I asked somberly.

She kept staring at the golden bracelet around her wrist. Her index finger and thumb rubbing the metal. She exhaled audibly and leaned her head against the headboard, her green eyes taking me in.

"They killed my protector. He wore this to ensure his longevity, but the moment they removed it he weakened. Then they beat him trying to get me to do what they wanted."

I had so many questions but didn't want to interrupt her. She was talking, and I was here to listen. I nodded when she looked at me again, so she knew to continue.

Jane winced when she moved, and more blood pumped out of her wound. "The man who captured me wants my golden feathers. That's why I'm the last of my kind. Our feathers are worth a lot, whether sold for the gold or crushed and used for medicinal purposes. But what Rhett really wanted, was for me to change into my human form so he could mate with me."

My blood boiled. A sense of urgency washed over me, and I wanted to kill this guy. No man should force a woman.

"I see I've upset you."

"I'm sorry." I rubbed my face and scratched my beard. "It's just I can't stand it when men behave that way. It sets a pretty grim picture on all of us," I said, my anger receding. "I've done plenty of things I'm not proud of, but that's not one of them. How long were you in hawk form?" It could explain why she couldn't walk when I'd first found her.

Jane told me how Rhett had attacked and killed most of her people. She and Michael, her protector, escaped soon thereafter. They stayed in the forests and traveled by foot as they lived off the earth. To avoid detection, she dressed like a man. Michael even cut her long hair off. She dressed in old clothing not to attract any attention, and they stuck to the shadows. They finally reached the rest of her people, where they continued living in fear.

She secretly hunted in her hawk form, but only once or twice a week. Her protector ensured her safety and when she transformed back into human form, he assisted her and ensured she rested soon after.

Rhett attacked her village six weeks ago and captured the rest of her people. He'd told her he'd killed everyone because she didn't turn into her human form.

It was heartbreaking to think she lived like this. In today's world where were-animals, vampires, and other supernatural beings roamed the streets freely, yet she couldn't. There wasn't anyone else like her she could go to for solace. Michael was all she had—and now he was gone.

Something brewed within my chest, telling me I needed to keep her safe. I wanted to ignore the feeling, but I couldn't.

Jane continued speaking, bringing me out of my thoughts as she described the size of her hawk. It impressed me, especially how fifty percent of her feathers were golden. But they would only be bright yellow if she was happy. While in captivity, her feathers had faded, and she had weakened. This angered Rhett, the leader, and he ensured she suffered by tormenting her slowly while they tortured Michael to death.

When she stopped speaking, her face had paled and her cheeks had sunken in. She was weakening from the poison in her bloodstream. Her wound needed to be cleaned without shocking her system.

I didn't want to tell her about the hot spring outside and its healing capabilities, but I had to. I couldn't allow her to suffer when I had the means to help her. Besides, she had trusted me with her secret. The least I could do was trust her and hopefully save her life.

I dropped the book and approached her. My movements frightened her, and she tried to push me away.

"I know you don't know me very well, but trust me. I'm going to pick you up and take you outside." I reached for her so she could see I wanted to pick her up and not strangle her. "Let me help," I whispered.

She nodded.

I picked her up, and she was even lighter than what she was when I first carried her. My hands felt the wetness of her blood as she nestled her head in my neck; the movement eased the tension between my shoulders and I leaned against her head, hopefully comforting her.

I kicked open my cabin front door and descended the stairs. Mist surrounded the area and over the small pond, a short distance away. The smell of petrichor in the air and I knew the storm was heading this way sooner than I'd thought. We had storms twice a year but there was a delay this year, and I sensed this one was going to be a bad one.

"Where are you taking me?" she whispered, her tone gentle and weak.

"I'm going to climb into a hot spring. It's hot so don't freak out but it will help, or I hope it will."

Jane nodded and relaxed against me. The smell of flowers wafted in the air and I breathed her in. Something switched inside me, and I wanted to keep her against me, never letting her go. My overwhelming need to protect her so strong—it was something I'd never experienced before.

I climbed us into the hot spring and sat down with her in my lap. The sound effects coming from Jane, from the sudden change in sensations, made me smile. At least I wasn't the only one who reacted that way when I climbed inside—and I was human.

Jane's body had been ice cold and the heat of the water no doubt took her breath away. When I was content she was still conscious, I reluctantly let go of her and gently sat her on a rock beside me. I helped her lean back and watched her expression change; the lines between her eyes flattened out and her mouth opened as she exhaled and relaxed. Her short hair plastered against her forehead with sweat and I moved a strand out of her eye.

"Hold on to me so you don't drown," I said, with humor in my tone.

She smiled weakly as her delicate fingers curled around

my bicep. I leaned beside her and felt her shiver in the heated water.

Jane closed her eyes, her lips changing from blue to red. Her cheeks blossomed into a healthy shade of red as the hot spring did what it did best—heal.

My smile reached my eyes.

The wound on her shoulder wasn't in the water, so I cupped my palm and poured water over it. Jane's eyes shot open. When she saw it was only me, she relaxed again.

"Thank you, this is... I don't know what it is, but it's magical. It has healing abilities I'd never heard of. It's wonderful." She exhaled, her breath caressing my cheek. I had to stretch over her to cup water on her shoulder, my face close to hers. In the moonlight, she was beautiful. Especially now that her color had returned and she no longer on death's door.

"How are you feeling?"

"Ah, so good. Thank you, Byron." Her eyes opened. "Thank you for trusting me with this." She smiled sincerely. "I can imagine how people would fight for this slice of heaven."

"I thought it was only fair since you've shared your secret with me."

Our faces were inches apart. Her green/brown eyes flitted from my eyes to my lips. I wanted to lean closer and kiss her. I felt the need to kiss every inch of her body. As much as I wanted to touch her, I wouldn't take advantage of an ill woman. But the instant pull towards her was so great I didn't want to deny her. My chest rose and fell as I moved closer. My lips inches away from hers. Her breath warm against my face. Her eyes darkened as her breathing labored. We were so close.

I cleared my throat and leaned back. I thought of math

and accounting so that I forgot about her lips, her skin, and her body.

"Maybe sink down until the water covers your wound." I offered, still cupping water over the wound.

Jane did as suggested. *Oooh* sounds came from her and she closed her eyes once more.

My head tingled and sweat beaded my forehead. Weakness engulfed me as I struggled in the heated water. "I'm getting out, but I'm not going far. I'll dry off and fetch another towel for you. Unfortunately, I only keep one out here."

Jane nodded, but said nothing. I think she was enjoying the hot spring too much.

I climbed out, shivered, and removed my shirt. When I removed my pants, I couldn't explain it, but I felt her eyes on my ass. I grabbed the towel and turned around. She quickly closed her eyes with a thin smile playing on her face. She'd just seen me naked and I couldn't care less. I wanted to remove the towel, so she saw all of me if it pleased her. And I wanted to please her.

A smile split my face in two as I watched her soak in the hot spring and wrapped the towel around my waist.

The light drizzle had stopped, but the storm clouds drew closer.

I twisted my clothing to get the water out and padded barefoot up the stairs to my the cabin.

Chapter Five

JANE

I could tell Byron looked after his body. When he climbed out of the hot spring, I couldn't stop myself from watching him undress. And he didn't seem to mind me staring as he dried his honed body. Luckily the rain had stopped or drying would've been for nothing.

When I first arrived, I didn't pay any attention to what he looked like. All I thought about was the pain and losing Michael; losing my people. That I'd never make it out alive.

Now that I felt stronger and my mind no longer cloudy. I saw him for the first time. He was ruggedly handsome, with a powerful body and arms. He wasn't big or bulky, but strong.

When he carried me to the hot spring, and being so close, I smelled the detergent on his clothing along with other smells. I detected little deodorant, with hints of sweat from an active day. And then the smell of him; a smell I couldn't decipher, but it was his scent—one I wouldn't forget.

Being in his arms and so close to his chest, I felt the heat from his body. It was comforting. I felt safe for the moment.

I averted my gaze when he turned around, but continued drying. A smile played on his lips, knowing I'd been watching him.

There's no doubt in my mind being a marine had helped keep him in shape. Byron had told me he had built the cabin himself and had already lived here for a few years, yet it still looked like he trained every day. I guessed when one lived alone there wasn't much to do but focus on oneself.

The hot spring was heaven sent. I moved in the heated water as it pumped out of the sides of the rocky wall like jets. The hot spring had a distinguishing smell to it I couldn't place; it wasn't the usual eggy odor, but a more clean, mineral smell.

If Byron hadn't shared his secret place with me, I wouldn't have felt the difference. While lying on his bed, I felt weak and nauseated. I thought it was from blood loss, but it was more than that weakening me.

The moment Byron sat me down in the hot water, I immediately felt the poison seep from my body. It was a strange sensation; like hot molten lava burning through my veins and seeping out my pores.

Although I hadn't healed completely, I no longer felt as fragile as I did before he placed me inside the hot, healing water. That's when I knew something else had happened, even though Byron had already suggested they had poisoned me.

I couldn't believe Captor Two had used a poisonous arrow on me. Rhett had probably instructed him to do so, but still. When I found him—*them*—I'd remove their eyes, then their tongue, then pick at their soft belly.

My stomach grumbled again. I needed to eat. If I wanted to shift, I needed more energy. The steaks Byron had made were delicious, and I wondered if he'd fry another two.

After a few minutes, Byron returned with a towel and a robe. He wore a gray V-neck jersey with holes in the bottom, sweatpants, and a friendly smile. The V-neck of the jersey was low enough that I saw his pec muscles bunch as he moved.

"Here you go," he said, placing the items near the hot spring. "How are you holding up?"

"Much better, this spring works wonders."

I opened my mouth to ask for more steak, but his broad smile shut me up. His dark hair moved into his honey-brown-colored eyes with some hair so long it curled over his ears. He combed his fingers through his hair that's in desperate need of a cut.

When he scratched his beard, I noticed that too needed a trim.

At the angle he stood, the moonlight highlighting his features, I noted he'd broken his nose a few times and had healed slightly askew, but it only made him more attractive —he wasn't perfect, and neither was I. His dark eyes held secrets I could only imagine. And although he was human, there was something about him I couldn't ignore; what that was, I was yet to discover.

I could tell he'd seen worldly things. Whether it was the hardness of his eyes or the way he carried himself. It was things no human should ever have seen. Yet he was taking care of me—a stranger—and not once had he asked for payment. He didn't seem selfish or mean. I knew everybody had their flaws, and I was sure he had them. But for now, I'd take pleasure in him helping me. Once strong enough, I'd see if I could return the favor.

My stomach rumbled again.

Byron arched an eyebrow with a sly grin. "Are you hungry again?"

I nodded, my cheeks heating.

"Two more?"

"Yes, please, I'm sorry if I'm eating all your meat—"

"Don't worry about it. I can always hunt for more."

He didn't wait for my reply and headed back towards the cabin. I heard the pan on the gas stove, the fridge opening and closing, along with packets rustling. Then I smelled my steaks along with that sizzling sound. My mouth salivated.

I appreciated the healing water cleansing my body, making me whole again. My shoulder itched, letting me know it was healing. I removed the bandage, and it had stopped bleeding, but a tiny hole was still there. It might take time to flush the poison out of my system. And I hoped by shifting into my hawk it would heal me quicker.

Now that I felt more human than a corpse, it was the perfect time to shift. I climbed out the hot spring, the cool air caressing my flesh. A fog had rolled in and thickened during the time I was outside. The smell of rain heavy in the air.

Once I stood on the grass, I rounded my shoulders. The wound ached and pulled, but it didn't start bleeding again, which I was grateful for.

I removed the wet clothing, wrung the water out, and placed them on a nearby rock. I closed my eyes and went to the gray place to call my hawk. She was there, her big yellow eyes pleading with me to set her free. She waited, but she couldn't come forward. Squeezing my eyes tight, I focused on her, called to her, but it felt as though a glass window was blocking her from coming towards me. I metaphysically reached out to her, touching a barrier, and a coldness spread through my hand and travelled up my arm and into my shoulder. I pulled my hand back and my eyes shot open. We couldn't shift. Something was preventing us.

"Is everything okay?"

I flinched at Byron's voice. My chest rose and fell as I tried to steady my breathing, but it wasn't working. My body numb at the thought of not shifting into my hawk. Nothing had ever prevented me from doing that. Shifting into my hawk was as natural to me as walking with two legs. Being blocked from reaching my animal was one of the worst things to happen to me—right up there with losing my people... and Michael.

I knew it was the poison doing this. It was obvious it was blocking me from shifting. I wanted to scream my frustrations. I wanted to give in to the pain. Give in to my captors and allow them to do with me as they pleased.

But I couldn't. The stubbornness in me refused to give up. I would heal from this. And I'd go after them.

It made me wonder whether Captor Two wanted to keep me in my hawk form or as a human. The more I thought about it, the more I realized I was easier for them to track if I remained in my human form. If Rhett and his men were on my trail, I needed to get away from Byron as soon as possible.

Lightning sounded in the distance, followed by a bright light. I glanced at Byron, who stood like a statue on his porch, staring at me. Not understanding why he didn't come down the stairs when I realized I was naked. Quickly I reached for the towel and dried, then slipped on the robe.

"Perhaps eat inside. It's going to rain soon," Byron said mechanically, leaving me outside.

I picked up my wet clothing and hurried up the stairs when it started drizzling.

"Where can I leave the wet clothing?"

Byron placed the plate on the small table and approached me. There was something about his expression I couldn't read. He took the wet items from me. His fingers burned the skin where he touched and approached the closed door on the far side of the kitchen. I watched him hang up the clothing on a drying rack inside the laundry room, followed by him opening and closing the door and joining me at the dining table.

We sat at the small two-seater dining table while I ate my steaks. The silence between us heavy, but not uncomfortable.

Now that I was aware of my surroundings, I glanced around the cabin between each bite. It was a large open area where the kitchen, dining room, and parlor joined. The living area/parlor had a three seater couch opposite the front door. Against the far wall sat a one seater under the small window near the front door.

A door leading to the laundry room, another for his room, and the last door, which I assumed was the bathroom.

A staircase stood against the far wall of the parlor, leading to an opening that stretched across the rooms. I wondered what he kept there.

"It's an area where I keep additional blankets or anything that needs storing," he said with a smile. He'd obviously seen where I was looking and answered my question without my asking.

I smiled and had another bite.

"How are the steaks?"

"Delicious," I said while chewing. "Fresh."

"It's from my kill from earlier today," he said, then had a sip of water from his glass. "I only hunt when I need to."

I nodded my understanding. We only hunted for food, never for sport.

Byron glanced at his bedroom, then after a brief pause he added, "We have a problem."

I stopped chewing, waiting for the other shoe to drop.

"Your blood seeped into the mattress and I don't think either of us should sleep on it. While you were in the hot spring, I've ordered another mattress and some clothing for you. The mattress will take some time but your clothing should come with the next food delivery."

"Thank you, but I don't think I'll be staying that long." I appreciated everything he did for me, but I didn't want to stay here longer than I had to. I wanted to leave by morning.

Byron gave a curt nod, stood, and opened the door to the laundry room. He came back out carrying linen. "Stay for as long as you like. Take the couch and I'll grab the floor—"

"I can sleep on the floor—"

"No, I insist. Really, I don't mind." He approached the couch with the blankets and pillows.

"Thank you." I thought it best not to argue with the man or we'd quarrel until morning.

I yawned.

Lightning flashed outside the kitchen window, then a cloudburst as rain pelted the cabin. The rhythmic sounds of water beating a drum as the drops hit the roof.

I finished my steaks so I could help Byron, but when I stood up, he had already covered the couch with a sheet and left a pillow and blanket for me. "Thanks for the steaks. They were exquisite." I rubbed my stomach and meant it.

"Good," he said, one side of his mouth turned up. He unrolled a sleeping bag near the front door.

"Are you sure you don't want cushions from the couch?"

"No, I've slept on worse."

I didn't know how to respond so I kept quiet for a few seconds then asked, "Can I use your bathroom?"

"Sure, it's that door." He pointed at the door I'd correctly assumed was the bathroom and entered.

There wasn't a lock on the door, but the handle turned and clicked when closed. The quaint bathroom had a bath and shower in one, a toilet, and basin. The furnishings were rustic and suited the wooden cabin. There was a stack of towels on one shelf, with various toiletries on another. No razor blades. I wondered if that was intentional or if he always had a beard.

Once done, I opened the robe and glanced at my shoulder in the mirror. The wound had stopped bleeding but hadn't completely healed; around the small wound, my skin was an angry red and tender to the touch. The dip in the hot spring saved me. I was sure I'd have bled out if Byron didn't share his little healing treasure with me.

Hopefully, I could shift into my hawk and heal completely. The sooner I left Byron in peace, the better. I didn't want Rhett invading his place after everything he'd done for me. I didn't want another death on my conscience.

When I opened the bathroom door, one candle on the coffee table bathed the cabin in a dim light. Rumblings echoed inside the room from the storm above us, reminding me of the time Michael and I sheltered in a cave when a storm halted our trek.

"In about five minutes, the bathroom light will go off. I

switched off the generator to save power. My cabin is off the grid and I don't use any fuel. Everything is solar powered but depending on the weather, it won't last long. If you need the bathroom during the night, use the flashlight." He pointed at the flashlight on the table closest to me. "If you hear strange sounds, wake me. But I'll probably wake up, anyway; being a light sleeper and all." He settled further into the sleeping bag and closed his eyes.

Lightning flashed, bathing Byron's features in bright light, forming dark shadows and sharp features. I climbed under the blanket, turned to lie on my left-hand side, and tried to get comfortable.

Although the poison wasn't as bad as it was, I still felt something. Like an irritation you couldn't ignore. I rubbed my shoulder, feeling the entry and exit wounds. My skin was sensitive and soft, but definitely healing.

I settled onto the couch, pulled the blanket tighter against my body, and closed my eyes.

The screams awoke me. The smell of hair and flesh burned my nostrils. My village was under attack, and I needed to help. Michael entered my tent, his face ashen, and he slowly shook his head, silently informing me there was nothing I could do. My people were being taken, and I was next.

"I have to get you out of here," he whispered, crouching near my bed.

"What happened?" I asked, climbing out of bed and slipping on my boots. I slept in my clothing in case I needed a hasty get-away.

This wasn't the first time they'd attacked us. I doubted it would be the last. Not until they had us all. They had captured some of my people. Now we were only a handful left. Being their queen leader, I was supposed to protect my people. But I'd failed. Being their leader meant it was my job to protect each one. But we were losing this battle. I could no longer wear my crown with pride. Not until the threat was neutralized.

Our numbers were dwindling and as heartbreaking as it was, I needed to survive or my people would become a statistic in a text book —a textbook that hadn't even heard of us yet. There were no pictures of us or information we shared with humans. We wanted it that way, but I see the error of our ways. It would be as if we never existed.

Our kind was being hunted like elephants and rhinos. While they were being slaughtered for their tusks and horns, they captured and killed us for our feathers.

Our feathers were used for medicinal purposes even though it was possible to keep us alive and still benefit. But they wouldn't listen, they wouldn't reason with us and we escaped. We had to hide. The difference between us and the other animals, we didn't have an organization backing us or keeping us safe. We were on our own.

Whether my brothers or sisters were still alive, I didn't know. And I missed them.

Michael grabbed my bag and pushed me through the back opening of the tent. Outside, flames painted the dark sky red. Smoke filled the air like mist, followed by men on horses rounding up my people.

"This way," Michael whispered, crouching low as we ran in the opposite direction.

"My people," I cried.

"It's too late, Jane. They've taken most. They almost caught me trying to get to your tent. Judas cannot walk and is in a cage. They hurt Penne. It's too late for them. If they catch you, that's it for you and your family. Who knows how long they will keep you but I have a strong suspicion Rhett won't let you go."

Rhett was their leader and after me for a while. He had invaded my kettle deep in the forest when he was on an expedition, searching for a rare falcon. Instead, he found us. And since then he made it his mission to collect more of us. But it was always me he wanted. I was my kettle's queen. And he wanted me. He wanted to breed with me. I'd rather die than have him touch me.

Reluctantly, I nodded. If Rhett already had my brother and sister, there was nothing I could do for them. I could escape, search for their where-abouts and release them before it was too late.

We headed for the water, where Michael kept a boat for emergencies. We dashed through the tall grass and onto the old dock where our boat waited. It was a rowboat with emergency supplies. We climbed on board. Michael loosened the rope and started rowing.

We didn't get far.

A man in diving gear rose from the water like a nightmare, fought with Michael, pulling him underwater. Michael fought his way to the surface, yelling for me to shift and fly away. I had to go now, to fly away and he'd find me. But I didn't want to leave him. I couldn't bear to lose him, too. But I had to leave. I could fly above and watch where they took him, then follow.

I dropped to the ground and thought of that gray area where my hawk stayed in the metaphysical realm. I called to her and she materialized. She squawked. She was unhappy. But understood we were in trouble and needed to escape.

I felt her enter me like someone had breathed over me. My bones twisted, my tendons stretched, and I shook my shoulders. My arms became wings, my vision sharper, and when I glanced down I saw my feathered body and curved talons.

Now that I'd shifted, I flapped my large wings, and rose above Byron. The man who had risen out of the water had grabbed hold of Byron, and pushed him into the boat where he bound his wrists.

I flapped my wings harder, trying to go higher as I cast my eyes around the carnage.

I didn't get away.

A large net fell on top of me and I crashed to the ground. My wings caught in the net and too heavy for me to continue flying. My body ached and my chest screamed. No amount of screeching helped.

In the distance, I heard Michael screaming as they hurt him.
Heavy footsteps neared. Then I caught sight of Rhett—my enemy. He crouched down, his hand holding one side of the net.
"Make sure she can't escape again. If she does, I'll kill you myself. And bring me the cage," he yelled the last part. "I want to ensure she stays inside this time," Rhett ordered his men.
They brought the large horse-drawn cage closer; a cage large enough for a hawk or a human.
I kept still. Watching. Waiting.
Rhett glared at me; his dark eyes boring holes through me. Whenever he was near, I felt the evil coursing through his veins and beat against me. And now he finally had me. I would not survive. I needed to escape.

"I see you, Jane," Rhett said. His tone ominous and his dark gaze searching. "Now where are you?" His voice echoed in my mind and not only in my dream. "Are you hurt, my love?" He taunted, then laughed. "I can take away the poison, Jane. Now tell me, where are you resting? Is that someone's home? Are you in the city or forest?"

The last thing I saw were his dark, soulless eyes.

I jackknifed out of the couch, almost falling forced myself awake.

Chapter Six

BYRON

I settled in my over-watch position while my spotter sat beside me, detailing our escape route if required.

We're concealed between buildings with nature behind us. Laying perfectly positioned on my stomach, I needed to keep my target in the crosshairs. Not wanting to move, I pissed in the ditch I dug when we first arrived. My body ached after lying here for six hours, but I dared not risk the operation by moving.

"Target's moving," Paul said, maintaining visuals through his own scope.

Our target had moved a hundred million dollars' worth of pure cocaine, and we still hadn't received the order to kill. He was in the kill zone, yet we couldn't do anything. Yet.

A young boy about twelve years old approached him. He lifted his smaller hand, showing our target the hand-grenade. Our target nodded and looked up. He looked right at me. Christ, he'd known we were here all along. An icy feeling washed over me.

"Shit, he knows we're here," Paul said with panic laced in his tone. "Abort, we need to go."

"Wait! The kid. He's sending the kid this way."

"Neutralize!" Came the deep baritone through the earpiece.

"He's just a kid," I said, keeping my eye on the boy's movement.

"Now!" the voice in my ear ordered.

"Just do it," Paul said, holding his hand over the mouthpiece so they wouldn't hear.

The boy was heading our way. I needed to act swiftly. It was either him or us.

"What about the target?" I asked.

"First the boy," commanded the voice in my ear.

I ripped the earpiece out of my ear and focused on the boy. Sweat peppered my forehead and dripped down my back. I inhaled, waiting for my heartbeat to steady. I found that place I went to during risky situations and exhaled.

Paul advised the target was still watching us, no doubt waiting for us to make the first move.

The boy edged closer. He was a hundred yards away. Ninety. Eighty. He was closing in. I took the shot. One to the head. The boy crumbled to the ground. His hand opened. The grenade rolled from his palm. I raised my rifle to the target. He started walking away.

"Target?" I asked Paul.

"Now!" I heard the voice confirm from Paul's earpiece.

I took the shot. The target fell. The grenade detonated. Screaming pierced the air. A mother running towards the chaos. Her son's body obliterated.

My hands cramped.

"Let's bolt," Paul said, standing up and grabbed his things.

I stood, picked up my rifle and bag. I grabbed my backpack and followed Paul.

My skin crawled with fear or regret as it laced its hooks into me, threatening to tear me apart. I hated this part; the overwhelming emotions engulfing me at once; enjoyment, satisfaction, relief, hatred, fear, disgust, and regret.

It was a job. One I loathed and loved. I felt powerful putting others' lives in my hands, yet at the same time I grieved those I'd destroyed.

But this time… it was too close. We were almost goners.

And my people hesitated, which fueled my anger.

Halfway towards our vehicle, screeching above caught my attention. A hawk circling as we sprinted away from the carnage. The hawk continued, then closed in on us. We reached our vehicle, climbed inside when the hawk's talons scratched me.

I jackknifed out of the sleeping bag. Jane shaking my shoulders, most probably trying to wake me, and I ended up smacking her hands away by mistake.

"Byron!" Jane yelled. "Are you okay? It's only a dream." She sat back, giving me space.

I sucked in a deep breath and wiped my brow. My dream… had felt so real. It happened. My killing the boy and then our intended target. It was my last mission.

Christ. I rubbed my face and scratched my too-long beard.

We'd been back at base a few days when they sent me for psych evaluation. I'd attacked my commanding officer, almost sliced his throat. He'd known what we were walking into and didn't tell us. Nor did he advise us to take the shot before the boy approached with his hand grenade. It angered me. I hated him. I hated the system. There was too much wrong with the world. And I'd seen it all. I had enough.

I'd been doing it for some time. My commanding officer didn't take my attack personally, but he hit me before I left.

They'd approved my early discharge and although I had worked for the government, some of our contracts paid by other agencies and they had paid me what they owed. At least they didn't hold that back.

I had used the money to pay for my cabin, said

goodbye to my parents, and told my girlfriend to move on. I wasn't in the right mind frame to give her what she wanted—what she needed. We'd only been dating for two years and she was young enough to start over. She soon forgot about me and found someone else. She married my cousin, and they now had three gorgeous children. My mother still sent me regular updates. I didn't blame my ex for moving on or for choosing my cousin—he was a good man, better than I could ever be. And she deserved happiness.

Rain continued beating against the cabin, the gentle pitter-patter soothing. When the thunder rumbled and lightning struck, it felt as though the walls were about to collapse.

"How long does it rain for?" Jane asked, nursing her cup of coffee.

"A couple of days," I said, enjoying a long sip from my cup.

We'd both had nightmares. Both struggled with our demons and had woken around four in the morning. We didn't bother going back to sleep. Instead, I made coffee and offered rusks. Jane wanted steak. I grinned, a woman after my own heart. I told her I'd fry us some steaks after coffee.

"It worries me."

"How come?"

"I need to leave. I can't stay here much longer."

"Are you meeting someone somewhere?" I knew Jane was in trouble and couldn't stay, but I had to ensure her safety.

She stared at me, choosing her words carefully perhaps, I wasn't sure. "No," she said after a long pause.

I gave a curt nod. She'd told me about Rhett, but the

way she'd said it, I knew she didn't want me to get involved. "I can handle myself—"

"I know, it's just…"

"You don't want anyone else getting hurt."

"Exactly."

"I'm okay doing what needs doing, Jane, really. And stay here for as long as you need to," I said, thinking about what to say next. It wasn't as if I had anything else to do today or tomorrow. She was here, and needed help. I might as well be there for her. If I died trying, then at least I hadn't wasted my life. I was helping someone in need. "I have enough weapons."

"I can't let you do that—"

I reached for her hand. It was cold and smaller than mine, and squeezed gently. "You can and you will. Besides, you can't go out there." I jerked my chin towards the window, the rain and wind dancing outside. "And you can't shift into your hawk. Where will you go? How will you defend yourself? You'll become a sitting duck for Rhett and I'm sure he'll take great pleasure in hurting you."

I watched her swallow. Her eyes glistened in the dim kitchen light. I'd struck a nerve.

"I'm sorry."

"No, it's okay. You are right, that's exactly what will happen." She exhaled a shaky breath and had a quick sip. "Thank you," she added, glancing away, then wiped her face.

"We'll get him, and if we don't, we trap him here and set off explosives."

Jane's eyebrows shot up. "You filled your cabin with explosives. Really?"

"What do you think?" I said, leaving my answer open-ended.

"Are you serious?"

"As a blood infection." I glanced at her shoulder wound. "How is it?"

"Better, but like I said, the poison is stopping me from changing. So now I heal almost human slow. I don't suppose you have a hot spring under the floorboards I could use?"

I grinned. "No, when the weather calms you can enjoy another dip."

We continued drinking our coffee in silence. My stomach grumbled, so I removed the last of the steaks from the fridge. We had one carton of milk left, two eggs, and one roll. I was running out of food and although the food parcel meant to arrive today; I had a feeling something might delay that from happening, especially with this weather.

The need to hunt to sustain Jane's hunger was intensifying. I gathered she needed protein more than anything else to keep her strength up.

My computer pinged, notifying me a message had come through. The only people who had my details was the grocery store who delivered my monthly food parcel and my parents.

'Weather bad, food parcel delivered tomorrow. New mattress next week.' Paul was a man of few words, but got to the point.

"Do you want the bad news or the bad news?" I asked. I knew I had to tell Jane about our food situation.

"What's wrong?" She turned in the chair, her bright eyes shining more green than brown. Her hair now had golden strands that glistened, depending on how the light caught it. Yesterday her hair looked dull, almost gray. Perhaps her healing had something to do with it.

"We have enough steak to last us today. Our food parcel should've arrived today, but Paul, the store manager, said he will deliver tomorrow. I don't think it will happen though. This storm," — I pointed my index finger at the ceiling and made a circle, — "isn't going anywhere for at least three or four days. The pond outside needs filling and this storm will do that, but it will also hinder our ability to hunt. But, I'll hunt and ensure there's food for the next few days." I knew I should've taken more meat from the animal I'd killed yesterday. It wasn't as if I knew I'd be getting a guest. A starving and captivating guest.

"I will help you. I'm a skilled hunter."

"I have no doubt." I smiled. I knew it was pointless trying to talk her out of doing anything. She was her own person and had gone through enough. I wasn't the type of guy to put her in a position she didn't belong. And if she wanted to help hunt, I'd allow her, just as long as she felt well enough.

Chapter Seven

JANE

Byron's steaks were divine. We each had one steak and a fried egg. Although I wanted more, I wouldn't take the food off his plate. Byron was the type of man who would give me everything he had.

Once we hunted and had enough meat, I'd eat again. Eating protein kept my strength up and although I couldn't shift, I was feeling stronger.

After breakfast Byron gave me one of his spare jackets and a pair of boots. My feet felt lost in the large boots. It was better than being barefoot.

The rain continued to pour the last hour after we'd eaten. Although I didn't know weather patterns, I trusted Byron when he said he sensed a change in the weather and the moment the rain lessened, we'd be out of here.

True to his word, two hours later the rain had let up. While we had waited, I started reading a book while he busied on his computer.

To conserve power, we only kept the living room lights on. He didn't have a backup system should the weather worsen. If his generator and solar system ran out of power, we had flashlights and candles. I didn't mind. I'd lived in the wilderness for some time and without running water or electricity. Staying in his cabin already felt like hotel accommodation.

Byron asked if I could handle a rifle and I could. When the rain became less, he approached the wall near the couch and crouched down. I furrowed my brows as I neared; in a panel in the floor he kept weapons. He handed me a rifle and grabbed one for himself.

"Let me know if you struggle."

"Sure, thanks," I said, looking over the Remington 700. It was one of the most accurate factory rifles made, and this one was the oldest I'd ever held. "You look after your weapons."

"Yep," he said, checking his rifle. "I have ammunition in my pocket if you need more," he said, handing me some. "You ready?" I nodded. "It's about an hour's walk." He pointed to the side near the pond. "Are you up for the hike?"

"Sure am."

"Good. Let's go before it rains again."

Byron opened the cabin door, and a blast of wind knocked me back a step. I felt like Dorothy watching wind whipping the rain in different directions but without the ruby slippers. There's no way I'd flown in this weather or it would knock me all over the place. As a hawk I could fly in most weather, but turbulent winds would hurt. I glanced at Byron and thanked my lucky stars for his rescue.

I rounded my tight shoulders and felt the wound tear, followed by wetness spreading on the shirt.

"Wait!" I called and stopped. I opened the jacket and pulled the bloody shirt down by the collar.

"You're bleeding again." Byron set his rifle down and had a look at the wound. "You can't go out like this. If you fire the rifle, it might tear the wound open," he said, shaking his head. "I appreciate you wanting to help, but I think you should hang back and tend to the wound. It's still crazy outside, otherwise I'd suggest you climb into the hot spring. But not yet," he said. His expression filled with concern.

"I really wanted to hunt with you. Earn my keep." I tried for humor, but my smile wavered at the sides.

"Thank you, but I'd feel better if you took care of yourself, rather. Can you manage?" He jerked his chin towards my shoulder.

"Yeah, I'll be fine." I glanced down at the pulsating wound. Blood continued trickling, ruining another item of clothing.

"Keep the rifle nearby. Nobody should come this way today. If anyone does, shoot them first, ask questions later," he said seriously.

"What if they're injured like me?"

"Two injured shifters in two days is highly unlikely."

"True," I said. "Okay, what time can I expect you so that I don't shoot you by mistake?"

"By nightfall." He grabbed his things and closed the door behind him.

I felt bad. I wanted to hunt with him, but he was right. My wound would just bleed again the moment I raised my arms to pull the trigger. The best was to treat the wound and rest.

The wound stopped bleeding once I cleaned and added ointment, gauze, and another bandage. My shoulder felt tight when I stretched it out. Then it started bleeding again. At least now I knew what aggravated the wound and would sit immobile.

I kept only the parlor light on to conserve power and sat beneath it while I read. Byron didn't have a television or radio. The only sounds I heard were the storm outside; the rain pelting the roof; the wind howling near the window and the insects dancing outside.

Before I'd kept busy. Now, with only the quiet of my thoughts, sadness crept in. I mourned the loss of my people and Michael.

Visions of my people falling or captured by Rhett's men left a sinking feeling in the pit of my stomach. There was so much chaos that day. I wondered whether there was anything I could've done to stop them. In hindsight probably not.

When I escaped my cage. I couldn't search the building because all I thought about was getting away. Now I regretted not turning back. If only I searched for my people, I could've saved them.

Rhett had said they all perished. That I was the only one left and only he could save my kind. Whether that was true, I didn't know.

Then when I landed in the forest and shifted into my human form, I couldn't recall seeing another cabin and was sure Rhett or his men would find me, eventually.

If I survived Rhett, I'd search for my people. I couldn't remember where the building was located, but I had an idea which direction to go. I hadn't flown too far when I reached the mountainous area, and then my wing couldn't keep me airborne any longer.

I'd been reading the same page for ten minutes. I couldn't concentrate and didn't like that feeling of helplessness or unable to understand what I was reading.

I placed the book on the coffee table and opened the front door for fresh air. The rain pelted down; the wind moving the trees in various directions. I didn't think the storm would let up soon. At this rate, I wasn't going anywhere for a while.

Although I wasn't in my hawk form, my eyes were better than a human. In the distance I saw dark shadows move. It wasn't nature showing its violent side, but someone was there. Someone watching me or at least the cabin.

I slammed the door shut and picked up the rifle. My body trembled at the thought of Rhett's men out there watching me, waiting.

With my back against the door, my rifle in my tight grip as I waited for them to storm the cabin. As minutes went by, and nothing happened. I wondered whether it was all in my head. Since I'd just been thinking about Rhett and what he'd done to my people, that I imagined the dark shadow looming across the pond.

Needing to know for sure. I spun around and opened the cabin door.

Chapter Eight

BYRON

I didn't like leaving Jane on her own. The men who'd hurt her were still after her. My cabin was the only building for miles. It was only a matter of time before they found her here. But we needed food. And with this storm, I didn't think Rhett would find us so soon. Besides, I doubted I'd be more than a couple of hours and would be home shortly.

With this storm not showing any signs of easing, I needed to hunt now or there'd be nothing for us tomorrow. We could survive without food for a week, but Jane was already so weak. Every time her wound bled, it weakened her further.

And if I was right, snow might fall by tonight. I could only hope my hunt was fruitful before it snowed.

I traversed down the path I'd used yesterday, but instead of going near the area I'd shot the deer, I veered to the left as if taking a very large girth back around my land. I'd seen deer this way when I walked home yesterday, but at the moment I had seen none, although most enjoyed being in the rain.

The rain pelted down from all directions as the wind whipped through the trees, causing branches to sway. I clutched my rifle with one hand while the other kept my hoodie up and my jacket closed. My drenched clothing stuck to my body.

A twig snapped up ahead. I froze. I cowered behind a tree, peering around it. Up ahead, the thin veil of rain revealed three deer a few yards away. They chewed and being as sociable as animals were. It was now or never. I didn't have time to position myself correctly, but I doubted I'd get another opportunity like this again. They'd sense my approach and movement if I neared.

I leaned against the tree, raised my rifle, and aimed. The closest deer would do, and it was the biggest. I inhaled and exhaled, steadied my breathing and heart rate. I ignored the stinging rain lashing my face—I'd gone through worse and still took the shot. I inhaled. The smell of water and nature assaulted my senses. I exhaled. Once a calmness washed over me and the deer in my crosshairs, I pulled the trigger. The deer crashed on impact while the other two scattered, running for their lives.

I was grateful I came across the herd of deers so quickly, saving me from being out in this weather all day. I hurried to where it fell and took what I could carry. This time I cut twice as much meat along with the liver, kidney and heart. I had a great recipe for dinner with the leftover rice.

Once I'd filled my bag with enough meat, I washed my hands and cleaned my knife in a nearby puddle and headed back.

I passed the familiar tree at the edge of my land and my neck tingled. It wasn't the usual sting from the rain, but something else. Something was off. I was within seeing distance of the cabin and stopped at the edge of the small pond that's in front of my home. I scanned the area and the trees nearby. The rain continued its downpour. No smells apart from the dampness in the air. No sounds apart from the hard-hitting rain, rumbling thunder, and bright lightning.

To my right, something moved. Whether it was a branch from the wind or something else; I needed to enquire what it was and headed in that direction. I didn't know if those seeking Jane were here, but if they were, I wanted to hurt them. After she'd told me what had happened to her and her people, I felt an overwhelming need to keep her safe. To protect her. She had nobody else to turn to. Her protector had given his life to save hers. The least I could do was help her survive and destroy those responsible.

I came to a clearing with flattened grass—someone had stood and watched the cabin. At this distance I saw the cabin clearly. I glanced around. There was nothing else disturbed. No other smells apart from the earth and rain.

I stalked around the pond in the other direction. That way I ensured the assailant hadn't headed this way while I was on the other side.

The violent rain continued pouring down, stinging my face as the wind whipped it in different directions. I glanced over my shoulder at the area I'd just been in and stared at the forest beyond; nothing else caught my attention. Whoever had been here had gone. Unless...

My heart stuttered in my chest. Although I was already wet, an icy feeling washed over me at the thought of harm coming to Jane. I'd gladly return to that dark place. To the place that left me broken, not wanting to carry on. For her I'd do whatever was necessary to avenge her. Any man who touched a hair on her body would deal with me.

My thoughts caught me off guard, but they were true. She made me feel something again. She made me want to be better.

By the time I reached the cabin, nothing was left disturbed. The cabin seemed quiet inside. I crept around the outer perimeter. No sign Jane was in trouble. The curtains were open, and I saw her sitting near the window, reading.

My breathing steadied as relief ran through me.

I inspected the entire outside area, but there was no sign anyone had tampered with anything. Whoever had watched from across the pond had left. We needed to remain vigilant. At the back of my mind, I worried they might return with more men.

When satisfied nobody else was here, I entered the cabin, removed my wet jacket, and stepped out of my boots. I opened the backpack and removed the plastic bags I'd packed the meat in.

"Is everything okay in here?" I asked as I scanned the inside of the cabin. There's no sign anyone else had entered. My cabin smelled as usual, wood, gun oil and the recent addition—flowers; Jane's scent. She had been the only other person inside and the tension between my shoulders eased, but not completely.

"Yes…" she hesitated.

"What is it?"

"I thought I saw someone outside." She stood up and approached the window near the door. "Out there." She pointed in the direction where I'd seen the flattened grass. "They just stood in the shadows and watched me."

"Yeah, I saw something but when I checked it out they had already left." I placed the meat in the fridge, left the backpack on the kitchen counter and stood beside her.

"Could you recognize them?" No-one I knew would come here and survey my property like that. Those after Jane tracked her here, observing whether there was a threat before approaching.

"No," she said, shaking her head. "I thought they'd storm the cabin and capture me, but they didn't. Then I thought I imagined it all, so I opened the door to check and they had disappeared. But you're saying you saw something stood there." Concern reflected in her expression, and I wanted to put her at ease. I wanted to hold her and tell her everything would be fine. That I'd do everything in my power to keep her safe.

Instead, I nodded and said, "Yes, they flattened the grass where they stood. But they're gone. We're fine for now."

She seemed to accept my answer as we gazed into each other's eyes. A deep connection joining us. Then a feeling I couldn't describe tugged at my heart and I stepped backwards, breaking the connection. I didn't know what was happening between us but the magnetism between us strong. I'd never felt something for someone so quickly. It was almost unreal.

I needed to keep myself busy; during times of emergencies I had ways of securing the door and windows. And this was one of those times. I should've secured the cabin because of the storm, but my thoughts were on the hunt and whether Jane would be safe without me. I silently cursed myself for putting Jane in danger.

I pulled on my wet jacket and boots once more and went outside to board up the windows. I had an aluminium bar securing the door in place, protecting us from a home invasion.

Once I was content the cabin now secured, I needed to get out of my wet clothing. I removed my jacket, pulled off my boots, shirt, then pants. The cabin was warm enough to walk around in my boxers, but I didn't want to embarrass Jane with my half-nudity. Although I felt her eyes burn my skin, and I wished it was her hands caressing me.

To avoid doing something I might regret, I grabbed a dry pair of sweatpants and T-shirt from my room, but it didn't stop my thoughts of her and me naked on the floor. I felt guilty for thinking this. She was in trouble and my mind wandered to carnal pleasures.

"Are you warm enough?" I asked, avoiding eye contact at first, and crouched near the fireplace. "I can make a fire."

"I'm not too cold, but a fire would be welcome," she smiled, which brightened her face. "It's perfect for this kind of weather." She sat in a chair and picked up the book she was reading.

"It is." I couldn't argue with her sentiment. This was perfect weather to relax by the fireplace. Unfortunately, there were outside forces that posed a danger, but until that happened I'd try to enjoy my day. If not for me then for Jane's sake; she'd gone through enough. I wanted her to enjoy herself for a moment or two, and I'd gladly keep her company.

I loaded some wood and lit it. The fire roared to life, the flames angrily licking the sides of the fireplace. I towel dried my drenched hair and beard. It had been a while since I'd bothered to cut my hair or trim my beard and made a mental note to get that done. I probably looked like a caveman.

I never thought it necessary to groom as often as I used to, since I lived on my own. I had no-one to impress, although now... I glanced in Jane's direction and she was staring at me. She didn't glance away as we gazed at each other. The connection we shared earlier ignited between us once more; warming my skin like the fire behind me.

Jane stared directly at me, watching my every move. I felt like prey yearning to touch her.

"When last did you cut your hair?" She asked, setting her book on the coffee table. I doubted she read anything in the book, anyway.

"A few months ago." I returned the towel to the railing in the bathroom.

"Who normally does it for you, or do you go into town?"

"I do it myself, but I haven't bothered." I shrugged, returning the backpack beneath the counter.

"Would you like a haircut?"

My hand flew to my disheveled hair, to the strands growing over my ears and almost in my eyes.

"I don't mind, I can cut it if you like. Just a trim should be fine. I'll leave your beard, I think it suits you." Her green eyes twinkled with something I couldn't discern, and a desire within me flared to life.

I scratched my beard. That too was getting long. I rubbed my neck where a rash had begun. I usually shaved till the neckline area but I hadn't done that in a few months either.

"Come," Jane said, standing up. "Where's your scissors?"

"Are you sure?"

"Yes, I wouldn't have offered otherwise." She opened the drawer I'd pointed at and removed the scissors. "Remove your shirt, or do you have a sheet to cover your shoulders?"

"No, I usually just cut my hair in the bathroom before I

shower." I'd usually stand naked while I did this, but doubted Jane wanted to know that bit of detail.

"Oh, well then, remove your shirt and pants or they'll be full of hair and itch the next time you wear them."

I removed my shirt and sweatpants, grabbed a chair from the dining table, and sat down. I felt exposed under her gaze and I reveled in it. As her gaze raked up my body, that need stirred within, and my body heated.

After I'd built my home, the last thing I wanted was the complications a relationship brought. Being a marine did something to me. I rarely spoke about what had happened. I'd done things I wasn't proud of, even though they were my orders.

When I first moved here, I wanted to get away from the world, including females. But I missed the company of a woman. Her touch; soft, delicate, and delicious.

With Jane around, I felt starved for a woman's company and glad it was someone like her. I didn't know what I was missing until I craved her touch. I felt like an awkward teenager again and couldn't help but smile.

Jane touched my shoulder, and it felt as though she burned my skin—like she'd branded me as hers. I wanted to reach for her hand, kiss her palm but reigned in the burning need.

It was insensitive to have these thoughts after what she'd gone through and silently cursed myself.

Jane brushed her fingers through my damp hair, and every nerve ending flared to life. My chest rose and fell as my breathing labored. Her caress made my scalp tingle, and I didn't want her to stop.

I wanted more.

Jane touched both my shoulders, and I felt her heated breath against my neck. "Just a trim?" she confirmed.

I nodded, cleared my throat and said, "Just a trim and around the ears."

"Alright," she said, and I heard her smile in that one word. She removed her hands from my shoulders, and I shivered from the loss of her heat.

The fire at my front was comforting and my back cool, but when Jane stood behind me again, her heat engulfed me. I'd love to be cocooned with her; skin to skin as we embraced.

My boxers tightened as my erection grew. I didn't want to make it obvious by covering myself, but I also didn't want to embarrass her if she saw. I covered the front of my lap with my hands. My erection ached. What I'd give to feel her dark depths. If that didn't happen, I'd love to rub it out in the bathroom. Unfortunately, I couldn't think of an excuse to leave my hair cutting session.

Gods how embarrassing.

Jane continued trimming my hair. The sound of the scissors as she snipped the ends. The caress of Jane's fingers as she pinched hair between her index and middle finger sent shivers down my spine. Every time she touched me, heat blossomed on my head and travelled down my neck, spine, and directly into my aching erection.

If she continued at this pace, I was sure I'd come without touching her. My mind was so far up my own ass, I didn't consider what I was doing to myself by not having *any* relations.

Time passed quickly as Jane snipped the long ends of my hair. She worked delicately and with care. When she moved to the front to trim my fringe, I froze. My erection painfully obvious. I knew she saw it. I sensed her reaction when she stood before me. But what caught me off guard she didn't comment or excuse herself. She didn't seem embarrassed, and she didn't say she had finished. Instead, she pushed my legs farther apart to reach my fringe. She trimmed my hair and ensured the hair near my ears was shorter and neater.

Jane wore a pair of my smaller sweat pants that hung loosely on her. Her knees touched the inside of my legs, and I desperately wanted to hold her.

She didn't wear any underwear and her breasts moved without restriction and so close to my face. I bit down on my lip to stop myself from reaching for her pert nubs with my teeth. I licked my lips in anticipation.

While she trimmed my hair. I wanted to rub my hands up and down her legs, even if that's all I did. I'd probably get slapped in the face if I tried anything.

On the other hand... I only lived once. To want someone so badly with trouble brewing made me feel terrible about myself. Then again, the thought of missing an opportunity would haunt me forever.

I didn't know what I was thinking. I blamed instincts on what I did, but wouldn't change a thing. When my hands flew to her legs, she didn't step away and slap me. Her muscles moved as she continued working, as if I hadn't just grabbed her knees. When my hands travelled up her thigh, she didn't stop me, either. I wanted to touch every inch of her. Then do it again with my tongue.

When my fingers found her hip bones, I stuck my thumbs inside the pants and massaged the soft skin.

Her breath caught and her mouth formed a surprised *O*. Jane lowered her arms, her eyes burning with desire as she took me in.

We stared at each other. My hands on her hips, my hard thumbs rubbing her soft skin. Her arms at her sides. My erection—now larger—between us. Her gaze traveled down. I smirked. Her eyes widened.

"What are we doing?" she asked.

"Whatever you want to do," I said. "Or not do." I squeezed her hips and let go. The moment my hands left her, an icy feeling traveled up my arms from the loss of her.

"No," — she dropped the scissors and reached for my hands, — "don't stop." She licked her lips and swallowed.

Jane climbed onto my lap, straddling me, my erection digging into her heated core.

Christ, I was going to explode before I touched her.

Jane reached for my steel member and stroked. Her delicate touch sent sensual pleasure rippling through my body. And I was about to come. I struggled to hold it together.

"Aah," I moaned as her strokes continued in a delicious rhythm.

"How long has it been?" she said breathlessly.

"Years," I moaned, my eyes closing and my body humming. "I won't last."

Jane slipped her small, warm hand inside my boxers and continued stroking. Her touch soft, then hard. I sank lower in the chair, my legs spreading further apart, savoring the moment.

I dug my fingertips into her hips as I controlled her movements with my hands, mimicking lovemaking while her hand continued caressing repeatedly. Her right hand holding onto my shoulder.

I didn't last long. I came hard and in her hand. My boxers were a mess and I almost laughed, but a smile stretched my face instead.

I wanted to return the favor, but Jane had to want it. When I glanced up at her, her heated gaze told me she did.

"Let me clean up first," Jane whispered seductively, climbing off my lap.

She washed her hands, then I washed myself. When we returned to the parlor, Jane approached the couch and turned around. Her brows stitched together, her lips apart, as her eyes moved my body. Then her expression changed, becoming heated with desire.

"My turn," she said, her tone sultry, and my erection was back.

Chapter Nine

JANE

It relieved me that I wasn't the only one who hadn't been intimate in years. We'd been running for our lives and I hadn't exactly had the time to consider relations with someone else.

Michael had been my protector. I hadn't wanted him that way. He had wanted more from our relationship, but I couldn't give him what he craved. He wasn't the one for me, although I loved him.

I felt bad for taking advantage of Byron. Deep down, I craved a closeness I knew he would provide. The guilty feeling didn't last long.

I noticed how he stared at me; it was a look that made my toes curl. His dark gaze telling me I was the only person in the world—in his universe. I guessed being the only female in a secluded cabin was the reason, but it was more than just loneliness. Byron made me feel things—things I hadn't felt in a long time. And I couldn't deny my feelings any longer. I couldn't deny him.

When I first landed and shifted into my human form

and a man emerged from the shadows. I sensed something different about him. Then, the moment Byron picked me up and cared for me. There was an instant pull in his direction. It was real. And it was potent. But because I had an arrow in my shoulder and poison in my veins, I ignored the feeling.

I knew it wouldn't be long before Rhett came after me again. So I decided I would leap at the opportunity as it presented itself to me. And that opportunity did when I pushed Byron's legs apart while cutting his hair. I'd never seen such an enormous erection before, as I felt my eyes widen at the bulge in his pants.

My core heated and tightened at the sight of him, and he hadn't touched me yet. Oh gods, I wanted him to burn my skin with his touch. I craved his kissable lips on mine, and his body against me.

I'd enjoyed the company of men in my long life, but I'd been alone for some time. It had been many years since I cared for another. Michael protected me. That was his job, and he was good at it. No man had filled me with hope. Not the way Byron did.

If tonight was my last night. I'd want to spend it with Byron. I'd gladly give myself over to his needs and desires, as they were the same as my needs. He wanted me, as I wanted him; more than I ever wanted anyone before.

If Rhett found me tomorrow, at least I'd die happy.

I stood near the couch and pulled down the sweat pants, reached for the shirt, and pulled it off with a wince. Byron's brown eyes darkened as he stared at what he craved. My skin tingled as his gaze raked up my body from my toes. His eyes lingered near my exposed breasts until they settled on my eyes. His expression burning with hunger, a craving I wanted to satisfy.

"Christ, you're beautiful," he said, approaching with purpose. He removed his boxers, closed the gap until I felt his warm body pressed against mine.

"Do you want this?" he asked, his tone sultry, like velvet against my cheek.

"Yes," I said, nodding, my breath coming in short and shallow. I marveled at his sculpted body. I skimmed my fingers over each ab and for the first time I felt as though I had a right to touch him; that we both needed this.

"You're mine until you tell me to stop." His voice deep and throaty, making my arms pebble.

I didn't have time to respond. Byron cupped my face and kissed chastely. When that wasn't enough, he devoured my mouth. We tasted each other and I couldn't get enough of him.

My hands roamed over his honed body, and I quivered anxiously. I'd been a teenager once and nervous for my first time. This felt like that time.

Byron's hands dropped to my shoulders. His hands burned my skin as he caressed down my sides near my ribs, his thumbs brushing over the sides of my breasts, and I felt like a quivering puddle at his touch. He pulled me closer, cupped my ass, and I yelped when he picked me up. I clung to him as he settled his knees onto the couch and slowly lowered us.

"I want to taste you," he said seductively, and kissed his way down my body.

I arched my back as he kissed my breasts, my stomach and then each hip bone. When he found what he was looking for, he swore and licked my silky slit. He sucked my folds, licked and teased.

My heart raced in my chest. My skin burned with

desire, and when he inserted two fingers, I burst with passionate fireworks.

Byron pumped his fingers inside of me, his tongue licking me, while his other hand pinched my nipple. The confusing sensations sent each lustful wave through me like a tsunami, and I came hard.

My body shook from the aftereffects, my skin tingling, and I was ready for a nap. But Byron had other plans.

Byron moved on top of me, his erection pressing firmly against me. I felt him at my entrance and slowly, pushed the tip inside. He didn't go all the way in, instead he hovered above me as his eyes moved over my face. I got the impression he was memorizing me, or even the moment. Like I was burning the sight of him to my memory.

A shiver racked through my body. I needed more.

As Byron watched, he pushed into me. My pelvis rose to meet his and he slid inside, inch by inch. My breath caught in my throat, my lips parted and our eyes locked. This was the moment we'd been waiting for; *our* moment. Perfection.

I lifted my legs and wrapped them around his body, pulling him closer. Slowly, he slid back out then eased inside, filling me. He moaned when I did. I felt every inch of him as he worked his way deeper, stretching me wider. And so painfully slow. I thrusted my hips up to meet his thrust. I wanted more and needed everything he offered.

Again, he pulled out slowly, dipped down and kissed me deeply. He broke the kiss, but pulled me closer, his cheek against mine and gripped my shoulders carefully around my wound while I clung to him. His pace was slow and tender as he made love.

That's what this felt like; him being gentle, slow, even romancing me. As if he sensed our closeness without knowing what exactly it was that brought us together. I didn't want to dissect what this was, I wanted to enjoy it.

Byron deepened each thrust, impaling me repeatedly with his hard member. Our lovemaking echoing in the cabin.

My entire body vibrated at his touch, needing more of him. Our bodies entwined. Our arms snaked around each other with a layer of sweat covering our skin. Byron filled every inch of me as the sensations rocked into me.

My moaning triggered his orgasm. He stiffened, then started pounding without restraint. My body ripe with excitement, I cried out in satisfaction as my second orgasm struck me.

I milked him as each pleasurable wave crashed into me. His body tensed, then became uncoordinated as he sought release.

My body shuddered with lasting effects as he slowed his rhythm. He thrusted one last time then fell on top of me, half crushing me.

After a heartbeat, he pulled out and rolled onto his side. He pulled me into the curve of his body and kissed my neck as his fingers lightly caressed near my injured shoulder. His beard tickled, but I welcomed the delicious sensations.

I pulled the blanket I'd used last night over us and we settled into a comfortable silence. We watched the flames of the fire as the rain continued beating against the roof of the cabin.

For a moment, it was only us. For a moment I forgot about Rhett.

And for a moment I pretended what it felt like being a normal couple enjoying a getaway in our cabin.

I pretended I was enjoying my life with my mountain man.

And for a moment I was in love.
But all it took was a moment to shatter my dream.

Chapter Ten

JANE

I fell asleep in Byron's arms and that's how I woke up. He was so warm against my cheek and body that I didn't want to move, some strange emotion taking ahold of me. There was no magic binding us, only raw emotion drawing us closer. I didn't want to let go.

Lying nestled beside him, my palm resting on his chest and his heart started to race. I glanced up to meet his kind eyes and he smiled. For a moment we were suspended in time, only the two of us sharing a precious second.

"What time is it?" I asked, noting the storm hadn't stopped, but it was darker outside.

"About nine." He kissed my nose. "I don't know about you, but I'm starving. If you like I can whip something together with the organs I saved."

"Hmm, that sounds wonderful," I said dreamily. "Would you like some help?"

"I'd love some. And if you want I can open the bottle of red I'd been saving?"

"Oh, what were you saving it for?"

"A special occasion." His smile reached his eyes, his face bathed in a soft light from the fire. "And this is special enough."

"I must warn you, one glass is my limit."

His brows furrowed. "I thought shifters could drink whatever they wanted."

"I'm not like others. I think it has something to do with the healing properties within us. We rarely drink or consume medication. And we heal ourselves pretty quickly," — I glanced at the wound on my shoulder that had now fully closed, — "and we can heal others but that poison, whatever it was, was nasty stuff."

"I'm glad to see you've healed." Byron leaned forward and kissed my shoulder near the wound. His warm hands roamed my side, his fingers brushing against my breast, ribs, and to the curve of my hip before settling around my waist. I loved his hands on me. "What's going on?" he asked.

"Huh? What do you mean?"

"Your expression just changed." His eyes twinkled with humor. "When I settled here," — he squeezed my waist, — "your green eyes darkened and if I'm not mistaken you smiled."

His words brought a wolfish grin to my face. "I love your hands on me. It feels… fantastic." I lifted myself up on my elbow and kissed him. "This was wonderful," I said, nestling myself under his chin, wrapping my leg around his while my arm rested over his side. "And this feels good." It felt better than good, it felt like… home.

"It does," he said, kissing my temple. "As cliche as this sounds, but I've met no one quite like you, Jane. Setting aside your abilities and the fact that you're a hawk. You—the woman—have thrown me off balance. Don't get me wrong, I like it, and I really like you."

"Hmm, me, too," I said into his chest, breathing in his musky scent. Having him so close, his warm skin pressed against my cheek, filled me with hope. It felt so good holding him and have him holding me. It felt as though the pieces of ourselves fit together perfectly. I knew nothing was perfect, and nobody was. But whatever this was—was just right.

"Come, I can hear your stomach grumble," he chuckled lightheartedly and sat up.

I reluctantly sat up with him, his arm around my shoulder and my hands around his waist. I didn't want to let go.

He laughed and leaned us against the couchback. "Ah man, I feel like a teenager," he said, kissing the top of my head and squeezed my shoulder. "We really have to get up and eat."

"I know… just one more minute."

"For you, anything."

We sat in a comfortable silence and held each other. With him in my arms, I heard his heartbeat and felt the heat of his body. My arms moved up and down with him as he breathed. It was calming, and I realized I was breathing in time with him. Our bodies now in sync and it was the most beautiful thing I'd ever experienced. I didn't want to let go, but I needed food.

"Okay, let's see how you cook," I said, squeezing his waist and let go. I pulled on the clothing he'd given me while he got dressed. I stole glimpses of his body and stopped myself from reaching out and touching him again. He pulled on his pants and shirt slowly, his muscles moving with dexterity, and I wanted to kiss him all over. But that would have to wait. Right now, we needed sustenance.

I sat at the kitchen counter and watched Byron work.

He was quite skilled around the kitchen, and my eyes kept darting to his hands. His skillful hands were all over my body, and I craved his touch again.

Now and then he'd lean over the counter and kiss me or he'd bring me in for a hug. He was showering me with so much affection, it usually left me overwhelmed. Yet with him it was the most natural thing in the world.

He prepared a dish using the organs he'd removed from the deer; kidney, liver, and heart. He boiled the last of the rice and defrosted a roll. He cut the roll diagonally on top into slices without cutting completely through. Then he added garlic butter and grated cheese between the slices and wrapped it in tinfoil, and baked it in the fireplace. He pan-fried the organs and two steaks with oil, then added garlic and spices.

The smell of meat, chili, and spices wafted in the air, and my mouth salivated. "Hmm, that smells divine."

Byron grinned, making him even more devilishly handsome. Byron wasn't sex on a stick, but there was something about him that called to me. His nose wasn't perfect, but straight enough. His lips weren't too full or too thin, but were kissable. And his body was hard and flexible.

I knew he was a killing machine, but it was his eyes that drew me closer; the deep brown with flecks of yellow or gold that made me want to fall deeper. He'd easily consume me while I wanted to be consumed by him. As obsessive as I sounded, Byron made every inch of me tingle and my core tightened without him touching me.

"Now I really want to know what you're thinking."

I didn't see Byron move, as thoughts of him consumed me. He stood before me, pushed my legs apart like I did to him earlier, and brushed a thumb against my cheekbone.

"What's going on in your head?" he whispered, cupping my face.

"I might sound crazy..." I leaned into his palm, savoring his touch.

"I know crazy and you aren't it," he grinned.

"I was watching you cut, fry, and do all these things you're so good at and I couldn't help wonder how attractive you are to me." I felt my neck heat and then my cheeks, taking me back to my teenage years.

Byron stared at me for a heartbeat, then cupped my face. "Ditto, babe. You're everything I always wanted. Actually, you're more than I wanted. For the first time in years, my life is going the way it should. And it's all because of you."

I should've been happy, and I was. But... my thoughts crashed as I remembered Rhett was still out there somewhere. Whatever Byron and I were having would soon shatter into a million pieces, along with my heart.

"Wait, now what happened? Why the tears?" Byron said with panic laced in his words as his thumbs wiped away my tears. "Why are you sad?"

"It might all end soon. You might be in danger and then—"

"Shh." Byron pressed his finger to my lips, then kissed me quickly. "Give me tonight, then we worry about Rhett tomorrow. There's only a few hours left. If Rhett comes knocking on our door tomorrow, we'll deal with him then. Okay?" A flicker of nervousness flashed through his emotions, then he smiled; there was genuine happiness in his expression that made my heart swell with love.

I nodded, desperately trying not to cry. I could do that. For a few hours I could forget Rhett. And I would give myself over to Byron; to be in the moment with him. Whatever happened tomorrow, we'd sort it out then. I could do today.

"Today I'm all yours." I confirmed with a curt nod.

"That's my girl. If Rhett comes here tomorrow or even the day after, I'd gladly blow up this cabin with him inside if it means your safety."

"You can't mean that?"

"I'm serious. If it means keeping you safe, I'll destroy it all." He kissed me chastely. "It took me a while to crawl out of my hell, but I'd gladly go back there to destroy him and his men. I mean it, Jane. I'll do whatever it takes to keep you safe."

I stared dumbstruck at the man who offered so much of himself. My chest ached as my heart swelled with affection. I pulled him closer and kissed him with a fiery passion that sent a sparkling sensation throughout my body.

He moaned in our kiss, while my stomach made grumbling sounds.

Byron broke the kiss and laughed. "Someone's starving. Let's enjoy dinner and worry when we need to."

Chapter Eleven

BYRON

Dinner was a success. Jane smiled throughout the feast and hummed her satisfaction as she devoured her meal. She almost licked her plate clean she enjoyed it so much.

She helped me wash up and then ensured the kitchen was spotless. We seemed to dance past each other as we cleaned. It was as if we'd rehearsed it, but we hadn't. It all came naturally. We seemed to know where the other would be, maneuvering past and did what needed doing. It was nothing I'd ever done before, not even with my ex. Just knowing she expected my every move warmed my heart so much I didn't want to let her go.

Once we finished in the kitchen, we sat on the couch and enjoyed watching the flames rage in the fireplace. The rain continued, a light drizzle instead of the downpour we had earlier. I suspected it might snow and relieved we had enough food to last us at least a week. If we needed to stay indoors because of the weather we would survive.

Jane moved uncomfortably on the couch, as if she couldn't settle down.

"Do you want to lie closer to the fire?"

She nodded, beaming at me.

I fetched another light blanket and covered the couch cushions now on the floor. Jane added extra pillows from my bedroom, and when our makeshift bed was complete, we settled into each other's arms with the heat of the flames at our front.

Jane seemed to fit just perfectly in the curve of my body. The smell of flowers wafted in the air as I breathed in her scent. I wondered whether she washed her hair with flowers, or if that's just her scent. But when I kissed her shoulder, her soft skin against my lips smelled like roses. It's as if Mother Nature had molded Jane herself.

The moment was perfect.

We lay in that position, her warm body pressed against mine, and we watched the hypnotic flames.

With her leaning against my front, my erection pressed against her ass. Nothing stopped the need. I wanted her in every way possible; not only now, for the rest of my life.

My thoughts caught me off guard, but decided I would decipher them another time. Right now was our perfect moment and nothing could ruin it.

Jane moved, pressing her body right against my erection as my hands roamed her body. My fingertips tingled as I caressed her side, down her hips, then near her front. She opened her legs, and I groaned appreciatively. My fingers trailed under the sweat pants and found her secret spot. She was ready for me. When her hand moved behind her and found my steel member, I pulled her pants down.

Jane freed me from my pants and stroked my hard cock, moving it near her heated sheath.

"Do you want me?" I breathed near the shell of her ear, watching all the hairs near her neck stand at attention.

"Gods, yes!" she whimpered.

"I'm taking you from behind. It's going to be hard and fast. Do you want this?" I said gruffly against her neck, watching the little hairs there rise. I raised myself onto one elbow so I could position myself properly behind her.

"Uh-huh." She nodded as she continued stroking me.

I removed her hand and kissed it, then guided the tip to her slick slit. When I pushed the head inside, she gasped and started grinding herself into me. This was heaven. She was tight and hot enough to send me over the edge.

I edged in deeper, stretching her, forcing mewling sounds from her kissable lips. Once I reached the end of her, I slowly pulled back out, then rammed inside. I gripped her hip to keep her steady while I thrusted into her.

We didn't last long.

The moment her moans intensified, it ignited my core, tightening my balls, and the wave of sensual lightning struck. I plunged inside her harder and deeper.

Jane squeezed around me, milking me, and I released my heated seed. My chest burned from the heavy breathing. A layer of sweat coated our skin, and I didn't want to pull out. I was happy to stay inside her all night.

I kissed her back, my rough palm grazing her breasts as I slowed my strokes. Although I already came, my cock was still hard. It had been so long since I'd been with a woman; it's as if I was making up for lost time.

A smile reached my eyes at my thoughts. I'd happily stay here with her, making love all day and night. To learn every inch of her body and what movements caused what reaction.

"Hmm, that feels nice," she said. Her eyes still closed and her hand rested on top of mine.

"I don't want to separate from you."

"But we need to clean up," she said, with humor in her tone.

"That we do." I kissed her shoulder again and slowly pulled out. The coldness was sudden, and I shivered. Jane moaned when I stood up. "Come, let's shower and get back into bed," I said, proffering a hand.

We did just that. Once clean, we were back in bed in front of the fire, snuggling closer. A heaviness settled in me as exhaustion took over. Our breathing slowed down as we relaxed in time, our touch a natural sedative.

We fell asleep in each other's arms and didn't move until the next morning.

The rain had stopped, and snow had begun to fall. I made Jane coffee in bed and checked my emails. Paul, the store manager, had emailed early this morning that he'd drop off my food parcel himself. He promised he'd come even if it snowed. He knew my supplies were running low.

Jane used the bathroom and as I sat on the couch, she opened the door, her face pale.

"What's wrong?"

"I don't know," she said, approaching me, "but I think he's out there." She sat beside me on the couch and took her mug in both hands. "The last time he captured me I awoke feeling the same way. I can't describe it… I just… somehow know he's out there."

"Okay," I said, sipping my coffee while I thought about what we could do. I had weapons and ammunition tucked in various compartments all over the cabin. If Rhett stormed into the cabin, we had a way of escaping and trapping him inside while I blew the building to pieces. I'd do whatever it took to keep her safe.

Jane set her mug on the coffee table and leaned back against the couch. She seemed too distracted to enjoy her coffee and, while deep in thought, twisted the golden bracelet around her wrist.

She'd told me Michael had been her protector for many years, but shared little detail. Nor did she tell me exactly what it meant to be her protector.

"What does it mean to be your protector?"

Her eyebrows shot up, her fingers clasping the bracelet, bringing it to her chest. "Uh," she hesitated, glanced at the bracelet, then back at me. "Whoever wears this receives insurmountable strength, and lives for many years. I don't want you to feel you need to be my protector."

"What would happen if I was? Would things change between us or would it be better?" I wiggled my eyebrows.

Her eyes flitted from the bracelet to my face as she considered my question. "I've had two protectors in all the years I've been alive. The first one fell in love with my oldest sister and swapped bracelets so he could become her protector. They died in each other's arms the first time Rhett captured us. And Michael had been my protector since then, but there was nothing between us. I loved him, but not romantically. If you were to become my protector, Byron, you'll be tying yourself to me for the rest of your life. Are you sure you're ready for that kind of commitment?"

I didn't know if I would ever be ready for commitment. But one thing I was sure of, if I was honest with myself, I loved being with her and was sure I'd enjoy spending my days with her.

At the moment I had little in my life. My ex had

married my cousin, and they were happily together while I was here... hiding.

I'd been avoiding contact while I thought I needed isolation. But what I was doing was more harm than good. I was starving myself of affection and the love I deserved. It was hard for me to admit that to myself, especially after the trauma I had experienced, I didn't think I deserved anything.

I thought about what Jane had asked. Whether I wanted this... to be her protector, and perhaps I did. Perhaps this was what I waited for, what I needed.

I nodded. "If being your protector means spending my days with you, then yeah, why not." It wasn't a question. "I was wasting my time alone here, anyway. I'd rather go down blazing knowing I fought for something worthwhile and removed those accountable."

Jane lifted herself onto the couch so she was sitting on her legs and faced me. She removed the bracelet from her wrist and stared at it hesitantly. The reality of what she'd been through visible on her face. But there was hope. Hope that I would be there for her and we'd get through this together.

"Are you sure, Byron? If I survived, we could be together. That part of our relationship wouldn't change," she smiled, "but the moment I place this on you, you're bound to me forever. When you remove it you will become weak, your age will catch up to you and you will die painfully."

"I'm sure," I said, nodding. I turned my body to face her and raised my left arm. "Is there a ceremony or do you just slap it on my wrist," I grinned.

"I place it on your wrist then say the words binding you to me." Jane raised the bracelet towards me, then pulled back. "You must be sure, Byron. Do you understand the severity of what this means?" she asked again, her tone filled with emotion that thrummed through the room; sadness, hope, and fear. I felt them beat against my chest as if joined already.

"It means I tie my life to yours. I will be available to you whenever you need me. I will fight for you and I will gladly die for you. You will be mine, hopefully," I beamed, "as much as I'm yours. The attraction I feel towards you isn't superficial. It's intense and I'm completely wrapped up inside of it. And I've been waiting for you my whole life."

A smile crept up her face, and her eyes sparkled with unshed tears. "If you're sure," she said and reached for me.

But she didn't slip the bracelet on my wrist in time.

The front door exploded. The metal rod securing the door bent and cast aside. Cold air blasted around us, followed by men wearing black. Behind the two men, a man entered. His sinister smile split his face in two as he glanced from me to Jane.

"Hello Jane, I'm relieved to see you're looking well."

Chapter Twelve

JANE

Last night was magical. Everything about Byron set me alive, igniting me from within, and giving me hope for the future. I knew with him by my side anything was possible.

Everything could change in a heartbeat, but I was ready for what lay ahead.

Then when he told me he wanted to be my protector, I was happy and sad; happy that I'd have someone like him by my side, sad that they would target and hurt him. I didn't want harm coming his way. I didn't want another person's death on my conscious—I wouldn't survive. But, I wanted happiness. I sounded selfish, but it's what I needed.

Then it all came crashing down.

I didn't have time to bind Byron to me.

When Rhett and his men crashed through the door, literally blasting it off its hinges, I had to slap the bracelet back onto my wrist or risk losing it.

My heart sank to my toes when Rhett separated Byron from me. I sensed his despair along with my own.

"Don't fight them." I told Byron. I didn't think I could handle the loss if they hurt him. Even without the formal binding, I understood what Byron meant to me and if Rhett knew this, he'd use it against me. I wanted to get away from Rhett, without him hurting Byron. There had been enough bloodshed. I couldn't lose him, too.

Rhett grabbed my upper arm and pulled me towards him. He wrapped a coat around my shoulders and pointed at boots he'd brought with.

"Be a good girl, or I'll make sure your new toy suffers," Rhett growled near the shell of my ear.

I wanted to gag at his touch and sour breath; he repelled me on so many levels.

I exhaled a shaky breath and tried to get out of his grasp, but Rhett tightened his grip on my upper arms.

When I felt someone watching me yesterday, I should've told Byron we had to leave. I knew Rhett would find me—us—but where could we have gone? The storm had raged yesterday and if we stayed with others, they would be in danger. I couldn't allow more to get hurt because of me.

I couldn't fight off Rhett with so many of his men around, but I didn't want to go willingly, either. I wanted to escape, but could not shift into my hawk form to fly away. Then there was Byron; I couldn't leave him alone to defend himself against so many. It forced me to comply with Rhett's commands.

Rhett ordered his lackeys to restrain us. Then he pushed me out of the cabin first, where two black SUVs waited. At each SUV stood an armed man holding the doors open, with a weapon aimed at us. If I got away from Rhett, these two wouldn't hesitate shooting us.

Light snow fell around us with a chill in the air; if it

wasn't for Rhett and his men, the scene would've been romantic with Byron beside me. The pond glistened a dark blue, and the trees waved gently in the wind.

I shivered at the loss of heat and possibly losing Byron forever. An overwhelming sadness pulsed through me. I glanced over my shoulder, and Byron's hurtful gaze penetrated mine as I stifled a whimper. I couldn't allow Rhett to see what Byron meant to me. Thank heavens Rhett wasn't paying us any attention.

Rhett pushed me towards the first SUV while one of his lackeys shoved Byron to the other one. They were separating us. I might never see Byron again once we climbed into the vehicles.

My chest squeezed as visions of Michael's hurtful expression haunted me; I didn't want Byron to experience the same. It was times like these I wished I was a bear shifter or something larger and powerful. One swipe of my paw and I'd take someone's head off. Unfortunately, I couldn't even shift into my hawk.

I hated feeling powerless. It frustrated me I couldn't stop Rhett or get Byron away from his men.

Reluctantly, I lifted my leg to climb inside the vehicle when something whizzed past my ear. I flinched when blood splattered my face and the guard holding my door crumpled to the wet ground. I spun around in time to see Byron slamming his bound fists into the guard holding him, knocking him unconscious.

Michael had taught me some self-defense moves. On instinct and the overwhelming need to escape, I used the distraction to disarm Rhett. He stood close enough for me to knock his weapon out of his hand, and I lunged for him.

I wrapped my bound wrists around Rhett's neck, using him to keep myself upright, and kneed him in his chest. He wheezed as air escaped his lungs, and his dark eyes rolled into the back of his head. He collapsed to the ground with me on top of him. A pool of dark blood pooled beneath his head; he'd fallen on a protruding rock.

Rhett was filled with sinister magic. I'd seen him swipe his fingers through the air and sliced Michael's soft flesh. I wasn't sure what he'd do to me once he woke up. With him unable to retaliate left me grateful to the gods. I said a quick, silent prayer, thanking them for the help.

The need to hurt the man who'd caused so much pain and suffering consumed me. I wanted to exact revenge for those who had lost their lives because of Rhett's actions. I unwrapped my arms from around his neck and sat up.

Rhett remained unconscious, but as I stared at him, his blood slowly started receding, as if going back into his body. His magic healing him.

If I was going to do anything, I needed to do it now. I curled my fingers around his throat and squeezed. He needed to die.

I felt Rhett's bones crunch beneath my tight grasp, and I didn't want to let go. But hurting others wasn't something I did. I hunted small animals while in my hawk form, but only to eat. I didn't harm for sport.

Tears streamed down my cheeks as I felt Rhett's body convulse beneath me. His face turning a shade darker, then his body quietened.

My body trembled at the thought of taking someone's life, and I couldn't do it. I let go of him and stood up, wiping tears off my face.

Rhett was the worst of the worst. He killed easily, quickly and without remorse. But I couldn't do it. I was nothing like him.

I heard a constant whizzing sound and cast my eyes

around as more of Rhett's guards crashed to the ground, red staining the snow. I didn't know who was helping us, but they were saving our lives. He'd surprised Rhett's men, and they were on the ground.

"Byron!" someone yelled as they showed themselves from where they were hiding and ran towards us. A large man with a full brown beard and a big gut. For someone so heavily built, he was surprisingly quick. He reached us in no time, a rifle in one hand and a pistol in the other.

"Paul, oh my gods, am I glad to see you. Can you cut this off?" Byron said as he stood beside me. Blood marked his knuckles and splattered his shirt. He raised his bound wrists to Paul. "Paul, this is Jane. Jane, this is Paul. He manages the store."

"Pleased to meet you," Paul said, and sliced through Byron's and then my ties. "Let's go before more come."

Paul sheathed his knife and placed his pistol in the holster at his hip. He handed the rifle to Byron, then hurried in the direction I'd first seen him come from; beside a copse stood an all-terrain vehicle, with a large box strapped to the back.

"This is your food parcel," Paul said, handing keys to Byron. "I don't know who they are," — he pointed at Rhett's men, — "but you need to go. I killed some, wounded others and when they wake, they're going to be pissed."

"Where will we go?" I asked, glancing over my shoulder. One man near the SUV moved as he assessed his wounds.

"Go to my place," Paul said with a curt nod. "You know where it is," he said to Byron, who nodded. "The family is with my in-laws, so the place is yours," he grinned, his cheeks pink and green eyes the color of fresh spring grass. He was an entire head taller than Byron, and even his hand dwarfed Byron's. "I can stay with a buddy of mine until next week."

"Are you sure?" Byron asked as he pocketed a key.

"If it keeps you safe, anytime." Paul winked. "What about the guy you were strangling?" Paul asked, staring at me.

"I couldn't do it," I whispered, sounding disappointed in myself.

Byron placed his hand around my waist and pulled me closer. "It's not your nature to hurt others."

"I know." I nodded and glanced over my shoulder at Rhett and his men on the ground. "They'll need medical attention soon." I didn't know Paul and couldn't divulge that Rhett and his men would want to hurry back to heal. Rhett had told me he'd created some kind of elixir from my golden feathers which helped speed up the healing process. I swallowed hard at the memory.

If Rhett and his men returned to the place he'd kept me, then I wanted to go, too. I wanted to understand everything he did there. And if I found the elixir he'd created, I wanted to destroy it. It belonged to my people anyway. And while there, I would destroy Rhett and his men. I glanced at Byron, knowing he would help me achieve this.

Byron noticed something in my expression. "What do you want to do?" he asked.

"I want to follow them, and destroy it all; the buildings, what they took from me, and him." I glared at Rhett, who was still lying motionless on the ground.

Byron pulled me in for an embrace, resting his chin on my head. I held onto him, savoring his strength beneath my fingertips, his warmth at my front, and the calm of his steady heartbeat against my ear.

"I'll do whatever it takes to keep you safe," Byron said.

"I'll help you." He kissed my temple and squeezed me for a second before letting go. "Can you help us?" he asked Paul.

"You know I will," Paul said, slapping Byron on his shoulder. "If it means keeping ya'll safe, I'm your man. And besides, I haven't had this much action since our last trip." He winked, wearing a broad smile.

Chapter Thirteen

BYRON

We waited for Paul where he'd left his all-terrain vehicle. We remained hidden as we watched two men assess their wounds and assist Rhett sit up.

Dazed and confused, Rhett wore a scowl as he realized we'd evaded their capture. When he struck one of his men out of anger by slicing his fingers through the air, I stood dumbstruck. Rhett was some type of supernatural who caused physical harm on another person without physically touching them. The lackey clutched his neck wound, but it didn't kill him. Rhett's anger vibrated through the air and left them all on edge.

Good; I was elated witnessing Rhett lose his calm demeanor as his true evil side revealed itself. He was not a nice man. No wonder Jane was so afraid of him.

I felt power pulse in the air like static electricity, causing all the hairs on my body to stand up. Rhett tensed up as he ordered his men around. His rage clung to him like a dark cloud.

I brought Jane closer to my body so I could shield her

when trouble arrived. We stood and watched the events before us. She held onto my hand as if I was a lifeline, and perhaps I was. I kissed the top of her head and she glanced up with a smile on her face.

"Are you warm enough?" I asked, wrapping my jacket tighter around her.

"Uh-huh." She snuggled closer.

Rhett ordered his men around. I couldn't hear the commands, but noticed how frazzled they were doing as asked while nursing their wounds.

Unfortunately, we had only killed two of them, which they left on the ground.

After an hour, snow started falling harder and as the last man climbed into the SUV, Paul returned on foot.

"Take this," Paul whispered, handing me a radio, another rifle, and a knife.

"Thanks," I said and glanced over my shoulder. I could enter my cabin and arm myself with more weapons, but Rhett and his men had entered. I wasn't sure what they had done inside and wouldn't take the chance. They could've set up explosives or devices alerting them to our return.

"I've left my ATV at the bottom," Paul lowered his voice, "and will follow them from that side." He pointed at the pond, letting me know he'd be going wider.

I nodded. "I'm tempted to leave the food here but we might need it."

"Yep, we might need to camp somewhere. I've also packed two tents in case. Best you leave now before you lose them." Paul jerked his chin towards the last SUV.

Jane climbed onto the ATV while Paul disappeared through the trees and bushes towards his vehicle. I climbed on, reached for Jane's hands and pulled them around my waist; having her holding on to me would do for now. I'd much rather be alone somewhere nice with her, but the sooner we handled this situation, the better. I started the ATV and followed the SUVs.

I didn't know whether Rhett had a tracker watching us, so I continued at a safe distance far behind their SUVs and surveyed the landscape as we traveled.

They created the dirt road when I had all the materials brought through to build my cabin. I'd sold my car because I no longer needed it, and since Paul sent someone to drop off my monthly food parcel I no longer went into town. This scarcely used road was still visible after all these years, although overgrown with wild flowers, tall grass and the odd fallen branch.

As we travelled, snow danced around us. Paul had brought clothing for Jane that fit, and a warm jacket his wife no longer used. She'd kicked off the boots Rhett made her wear and slipped on the snow boots Paul had given her. At least she was warm behind me.

Paul brought me clothing even though it was too big. He didn't have spare helmets, but I wasn't going fast, anyway. We cruised slowly, ensuring nobody watched us following the black SUVs.

Jane tightened her hold; her arms snaked around my waist as she clung to me. I felt her head press against my back. I patted her hands clutching my jacket, comforting her.

Temptation threatened to pull me in a different direction. I wanted to drive until we reached the end of town. Where we could hide away from the world. But I wanted to help Jane and destroy everything Rhett had taken from her. While we waited for Paul, she'd told me about the elixir. I had to continue on this path to help her.

We continued maneuvering through the winding forest

until the SUVs came to a paved road and headed west. I couldn't take the ATV onto the road. Instead, we cruised alongside the road, keeping an eye out for cops. The last thing we needed was to get arrested.

The SUVs turned right at a crossing, heading north. We continued on the shoulder of the road. It relieved me we weren't heading for the interstate.

When the vehicles slowed near a compound, I passed and continued around the property to get a better look. Within the perimeter stood two buildings, one warehouse-type looking building while the other smaller and three stories reminding me of a house.

Jane flinched when she turned to see. "I think that's where they kept us," she said softly, her voice meek. Her body trembled behind mine, and I pulled her closer.

"We'll find a way inside and destroy it all," I said confidently.

"Before you do anything," she said, climbing off the ATV. "Here," she reached for my hand, "it will strengthen you and keep you safe." She removed the golden bracelet from her wrist. "Last chance to change your mind. Once this is on, never take it off." She warned.

"I want this," I said, meaning every word.

A grin crept up my face as she touched my wrist with her free hand while the other slipped the bracelet on. The cold band burned into my skin. When Jane whispered words I couldn't decipher my skin crawled, it felt like tiny insects biting into my flesh. My chest warmed as heat spread from the cool bracelet as it melded into my skin—it now looked like a golden tattoo around my wrist instead of jewelry.

A shudder ran through me as Jane continued her incantation. Her eyes closed, her warm hands on my arm as I felt her power pulsed through me.

I exhaled, and my breath crystalized before me, then melted to the ground. My chest rose and fell as a nervousness swept through me. A cold sweat peppered my forehead as sweat beaded near my neck. Strange sensations washed over me as hot and cold tingles brushed against my skin.

I opened and closed my hands as raw power surged at my fingertips. The muscles throughout my body thrummed with an unseen force. I felt... stronger... potent... and an overwhelming need to protect.

I glanced down at the beauty by my side and reached for her. She opened her eyes when I cupped her face. The force thrummed at my fingertips, and I was sure I saw blue sparks at our touch. She smiled lazily, yet her eyes filled with heated passion.

Christ, I came undone.

Her seductive gaze shot to my heart, and all my blood pumped to one spot.

I pulled her closer, our lips touching, and I felt her strength course through me like a bright golden light. It felt as though the gods themselves had blessed me with their power.

I devoured her mouth as she clung to my body. I never wanted to let her go.

She was mine. I was hers.

And this thing she did—joining us—was the best thing that happened to me. I no longer felt the constant sadness or my overwhelming anxiety. In its place was love and strength. Qualities she needed in a protector, but also as a mate. My mate.

"Mine," I growled.

Jane grinned as she reached for my pants, unbuttoned

and unzipped me. She shimmied her pants down and pulled me closer.

"What are you doing? It's cold and snowing," I said for her benefit than my own. I'd love nothing more than to show how much I loved and cared for her, but I didn't want her to feel discomfort out here with the elements beating against us. Not to mention Rhett and his men were nearby.

"I want you... now. I need you," she breathed. "I have to complete it..." She left her words trailing as her desire stormed in her bright green eyes.

This was going to be a quickie.

Jane turned around and leaned over the ATV, her naked ass waiting for me. I glanced around, but it was only us surrounded by trees and soft snow flakes dancing around us. In one swift motion, I plunged inside her heated depths and almost came on impact. She was so tight, hot, and moist. I wouldn't last five minutes.

"Oh gods," she moaned, pushing her ass out, meeting my strokes with her own.

I gripped her hips and pummeled her with my molten member. Her power continued coursing through me, and the joining of our bodies felt like the last element tying me to her. My chest squeezed with affection as I embraced her. Protected her. Loved her.

I wanted to feel every inch of her. I pushed her legs apart and thrusted deeper.

She moaned with desire as she continued twitching around me.

I slowed my coordinated and powerful thrusts. Jane squeezed around me, milking my cock. She moaned into her hands. But it only fueled my desire, and I continued that pleasurable rhythm.

When my orgasm struck, I grabbed her shoulders,

pushing all the way to the end. Sparks of pleasure burned throughout my body as I released my seed within her.

Jane shuddered, making my cock pulse one last time, and I fell across her back. Every part of me tingled, sparkly stars filled my vision as my heart pounded, threatening to burst out my chest.

"Hmm, that was…" Jane licked her lips, "yummy." She slowly stood up, forcing me to climb off her.

I pulled out and reached for my pants. My entire body felt light as a feather, yet powerfully built. The empowering sensations contradicting yet strange at the same time. I didn't feel like this before.

Jane buttoned up her pants and turned around, her cheeks a healthy shade of pink.

"Is that what happens to all protectors?" I teased, the twinge of jealous enveloping me.

"No, only you. I sealed the bond, validating you as my mate. The difference is, if anything happens to you, I will die too."

I gawked at her, my mouth opened in a surprised *O*. "Are you serious? You've just signed your death warrant."

"I know," she said, fixing her shirt and zipping up her jacket. "You're everything I ever wanted in a mate, Byron," she said my name so tenderly, it squeezed at my heartstrings. "If anything happens to you, I don't think I'd want to continue living. And yes, this is probably a suicide mission," — she stared at the compound behind me, — "and neither of us might walk out of there. But at least I will die knowing I have you by my side. My mate."

Jane was quiet for a moment, then continued. "I don't want Rhett getting away with his actions. He killed my people and he won't stop until I finally give in and breed with him or I'm dead. It hurts me to ask you to go back into your marine mindset, but I need you to kill him and those who work for him. I hate we must do this, but none can remain alive. They will just keep sending more men after us. It ends here, now," she said with determination stamped all over her face.

This was what united us; we both had reached a point in our lives where we had had enough of our circumstances. It was now or never. Where I'd given up on my marine life and built my cabin, living in solitude. Jane wanted the men responsible to pay for what they did to her people. As much as I didn't want to go back to that dark place where I killed, I wanted to. For her I'd gladly be the one to deliver Rhett's head on a plate and destroy the compound.

"For you, my love, I'll do whatever it takes." I promised, sealing my fate and most likely hers as well.

Chapter Fourteen

JANE

Something came over me. All I knew, as I bound myself to Byron, he was *the one*. He was my mate, and I was his. To solidify our bond, we made love. It was foolish to do it out in the open, hidden between trees and nature, but necessary.

My skin tingled from our consummation, and power thrummed at my fingertips. My hawk squawked within me. She was pleased with our decision. She understood our predicament, and although she was reluctant for us to storm the compound, she knew we had to.

I clung to Byron, never wanting to let go. He was the man I'd always been waiting for. All the years alone, I knew the right one was out there. I just had to bide my time. And here he was holding me, the one I dreamed of; sensitive yet strong, kind yet fierce, protective yet understanding.

I loved him.

We'd only spent a couple of days together, yet it felt like years. My heart swelled with warmth, and I knew it was our bond that secured me to him. I gave him one last squeeze and reluctantly let go. We had a job to do.

Byron didn't let go, either. His honey-colored eyes darkened as he gazed down at me, a playful smile on his face.

"I love you." He beamed.

"I love you, too."

We kissed chastely, which was cut short by a buzzing sound. We turned in that direction, watching Paul drive up the same path we'd taken. Paul had the same thought as Byron, driving around the perimeter, and coming across our little hideaway. It worried me because if he found us, so could Rhett's men.

Paul greeted us by tipping his head and killed his ATV. He climbed off his vehicle to survey the area.

"Pretty scenery but that," — he pointed at the compound, — "stands out like a sore thumb. Nothing screams villain like a warehouse painted black." He shook his head.

"Yep, there's been little movement, but they're all in there," Byron replied, jerking his chin in the compound's direction.

"Do you know which building they're in?"

"Probably both. Look here," — Byron pointed at the nearest cameras, — "see where they're positioned." Paul nodded. "This is their weakest spot." Byron pointed at the fence a short distance from us. "The cameras don't rotate all the way. I doubt they can see that side of the fence."

Paul glanced at the cameras and nodded. "Good call," he said, smiling. "And I brought enough guns, ammo, and even cutters." He wiggled his bushy eyebrows.

While Paul and Byron readied themselves with weapons, I practiced holding the small pistol Paul had offered. It was his wife's Glock, and Byron had shown me how to use it.

In all the years I'd been alive, I'd never used a gun with intent to kill another human. We used guns to protect ourselves only. We were not a violent group of shifter hawks. Those who fought used knives, sticks, or their fists. Then again, we never had to defend ourselves until Rhett came along.

"Are you ready?" Byron snaked his arms around my waist and said near my ear. The action sent waves of goose-bumps all over my body. I turned in his embrace, rocked onto my toes, and kissed him deeply. He smiled in our kiss. I wanted to get lost with him. To lie naked, exploring each other's body, and forget about the world.

Not yet, I thought. We had a job to do first. Then we'd do all that yummy stuff as long as possible.

"Yes," I said reluctantly. As much as I wanted to spend my days with him. I needed to do this first. Rhett needed to stand judgement for what he had done to my people.

We walked in a crouched position towards the fence. Paul used his bolt cutters to penetrate the wire fencing, and we slipped through. The sun had set. The chill bit into my skin through the jacket. But it had stopped snowing.

There were no outdoor lights alerting them to our presence, and no alarms sounded. We took it as a good sign that the cameras hadn't picked up our trespassing and continued towards the closest building.

When the two black SUVs first drove up the winding driveway, they parked near the bottom of the compound. The building we approached looked like a separate section and possibly where they slept. A triple story brick building with blinds at each window. We couldn't see in, but it seemed like the safest side to enter first.

The icy breeze caressed my exposed face. I slipped my hands into the jacket pockets to keep warm. Squeezing the gun handle in my pocket, my finger lightly on the trigger. I didn't like the idea of using it, but to protect myself and Byron, I would.

Paul stood with his weapon raised towards the door and behind me, while Byron picked the lock. When Byron unlocked the door, he carefully opened it with a low squeak. Byron peered into the vacant room while Paul covered him —both men with their weapons aimed at any evil-doer.

Once they were content nobody was about to jump out and shoot us, we entered. Inside was a small kitchenette and couch; on one side of the wall stood a table with used mugs scattered atop. I assumed this was their break room; trained soldiers needed to eat and drink, too.

The hallway was eerily quiet and dark. The walls a dark gray with dim lights, which barely illuminated the space.

I followed Byron, with Paul bringing up the rear.

Paul tapped my shoulder. I reached for Byron, and we stopped. Paul pointed to a set of stairs we'd passed. "I'm going up and will meet you on the other side," he whispered.

"You sure you don't want to stay together?" Byron asked.

"Nah, it will go quicker if we split up. I'll check upstairs while you see if you can go to the next building. And remember our deal."

Byron nodded.

When Paul left, I asked Byron what he meant.

"If we don't see him by the time we're ready, we leave without him—"

"No, we can't leave him here."

"It might cost us our lives if we go back to find him," he said, consoling me.

I couldn't argue with that. But leaving anyone behind didn't sit well with me. Paul had a wife and kids and agreed to help us without thinking it through. But he was a trained killer and knew the risks. That didn't mean I agreed with their plan.

I nodded, even though the idea left me uncomfortable. Byron grabbed my hand and we continued along the quiet hallway.

We reached the end of the hallway, coming across an empty room with a table and a computer atop. At another closed door, Byron paused and pressed his ear against it. Slowly, he opened the door, revealing another empty office.

The next door led us to another hallway, a stark contrast to the one we'd just left. This hallway had bright white walls and white tiled floors. The smell of bleach and citrus wafted in the air, reminding me of hospitals. This hallway had doors on one side.

We traversed the medically white hallway and stopped at the first open door. Inside stood a medical bed in the centre and a hospital screen pulled halfway. To one side stood a desk and chair. I shuddered when I saw the shelves; bottles filled with solution and different organs floating in each.

I pushed Byron to the next door. I didn't want to see more. My blood boiled with anger. If those organs belonged to my people. I wanted to burn this place down. These walls had witnessed crimes against my people and shouldn't be standing.

The next door had a secure keypad on the right-hand side. Slowly, we peered through the little glass window. On the floor stood large automated machines with moving parts where tiny vials filled with solutions, then moved like a train to the next section to be packed in boxes. It was a pharmaceutical factory.

My veins froze. My skin heated.

It fueled my rage to witness this. I didn't want to be right. Rhett had killed my people, extracting their essence to create a healing elixir. Then he manufactured it into those vials so he could sell it.

"I want him dead and this place destroyed," I said through gritted teeth. "If I die with them, so be it, just as long as we destroy everything." I pointed at the machines, my index finger hitting the glass window.

"What's inside?"

"Rhett has extracted my people's life essence and bottled it." When Byron didn't respond and the lines between his eyes deepened, I added, "Remember how I said we have healing qualities?" He nodded. "Rhett has used that part of our DNA to produce his product. In order to make so much, he's killed my people to get their essence," I said gravely.

"Do you think your people are still alive? Maybe he's keeping them alive to keep extracting."

I blinked my response. It never occurred to me they would still be alive, especially since Rhett had said I was the last of my kind. That he alluded to killing everyone. I knew I couldn't trust him, but I never suspected they would be here.

It filled me with hope, knowing my people might be alive. I blinked, shedding tears. I gripped Byron's forearm as emotions rocked into me. An overwhelming sense of relief crashed into me; the possibility that I wasn't alone, that my people might be alive.

"We need to find them, Byron. If they are still alive, and Rhett is extracting from them, we need to find them now," I said, my chest aching.

Byron kissed my temple and gave a curt nod, determination in his expression. "We will."

As hawk shifters, our emotions showed on our feathers. The weaker and sadder we became, the less our feathers shined gold. I imagined how they had deteriorated; their bodies bruised and broken.

"Let's go this way," — Byron pointed to the side, — "there're more rooms here and upstairs." He reached for my hand and I slipped mine into his.

Just knowing Byron was by my side filled me with hope. We could do this.

Slowly, we checked all the downstairs rooms, but they were empty. They all had that hospital ambiance, and in each room I prayed none of my people had died there.

We stopped near stairs and another door. Byron pressed his head against the door, then stepped back, shaking his head. He pointed up the stairs. I followed him. As we reached the next floor, the door we had left opened.

"Are you sure nobody breached the perimeter?" a man asked. His voice deep and throaty, reminding me of someone who smoked all their life. It wasn't Rhett's voice.

"No, I checked the footage but there's a blind spot at the back—"

"Go check it out. And next time something like this happens, I expect you to do your job. Now go!"

"Yes, sir," the other man said, his tone meek.

Footsteps sounded going away from us while the other footsteps climbed the stairs towards us.

Chapter Fifteen

BYRON

We didn't know how many men roamed the floor or how armed they were.

The man ascending the stairs was a potential threat, and I pushed Jane behind me. The footsteps neared. He breathed hard like he was a smoker or used to smoke, and now any physical activity made him wheeze.

"Yeah, hi," he said, most likely on his cellphone. Then his footsteps stopped. "You know I don't use that shit. Who knows what else Rhett puts in there because it certainly isn't pure," he said, then paused, listening to the other person. Since I was human, I only heard his side of the conversation. "Yeah... okay... sure," he said, then continued up the stairs.

As the man rounded the corner, I slammed my fist into his throat. He gagged, his eyes bulged, and grabbed his neck. The impact forced him backwards, but he didn't go down the stairs.

I smashed my fist into his solar plexus, rendering him

stunned, and he doubled over. I brought my knee into his face, crunching sounded and blood splattered the floor.

The man didn't have a chance. My movements were quick and hard. He wouldn't be able to breathe properly and in a world of pain.

Knowing my punches hurt him, I knew he was only human. With hands on his bloody face, I was sure his diaphragm was spasming as he struggled to breathe.

I followed with a punch to his jaw, snapping his head to the side. I didn't want him making a noise as he hit the wooden floor, so I caught him and sat him down against the wall to nurse his wounds. But I didn't want him coming after us again, either. Anyone working for Rhett was evil in my eyes, and I guaranteed he had hurt many people. He deserved worse.

"Look away," I commanded.

Jane stared with wide eyes, unblinking.

"Jane! Look away," I repeated.

She nodded quickly, then turned away.

I grabbed the man's head and snapped it quickly to one side; I needed him paralyzed and silenced. Although it took strength to break someone's spinal cord, it was possible. It was a slow and painful death; by crushing his windpipe he struggled to breath then by snapping his spine it left him motionless. But he would eventually die. And although it tempted me to leave him be, I would kill him humanely as possible. I pulled the hunting knife Paul had given me and sliced his carotid artery. He slumped over and onto the floor, his blood pooling beneath him.

"Don't look," I said, grabbing Jane's hand and pulling her away from the carnage. She did as I suggested. I doubted she wanted to see unnecessary bloodshed.

The second floor of the larger warehouse had doors on

both sides of the white hallway. The medically white paint continued here. A shudder ran through me when I smelled something other than bleach.

"Do you smell that?" I whispered.

Jane nodded. "Blood mixed with something else."

"Rotting flesh," I confirmed.

Slowly, we traversed down the hallway. I squeezed Jane's hand as her power continued coursing through me. I felt stronger, like I could take on everyone in the warehouse single-handedly. But I wouldn't be foolish. I needed to keep Jane at my side so that I could protect her.

We continued in the smell's direction. The closer we approached the door at the end of the hallway, the stronger the odor. I didn't know what to expect. It could be rotting corpses. If it was Jane's people, she needed closure.

"You want me to enter first?"

"No, I have to do this. I have to know what Rhett did to them."

I nodded my understanding and slowly opened the unlocked door. This alone should've deterred us, but it didn't. This was most likely a trap, that Rhett had somehow known we'd come.

I slowly opened the door wider for Jane and paused. My mind reeling with what I saw. Glass cages holding men, women, and children. Some stood as we entered, their attention on us. They remained quiet. Not even a child called for help.

I wondered whether they recognized Jane with her short hair.

When we reached the first cage, a man approached, placing his hand on the glass. "Queen," he said, bowing his head.

Jane neared the glass and placed her hand on the glass, mimicking him. "Josiah." She choked back a sob. "We're here to get everyone out."

"He told us you died." Josiah swallowed hard. He dropped his arm to his side, never once looking away from Jane, his queen. "We knew you were stronger than that. We knew you'd come back for us."

Jane wiped the rogue tear from her cheek. "Michael didn't make it," she said, dropping her arm. "Where's my brother and sister?"

Josiah pointed to the side. "The last cage."

I counted ten glass cages, with a mixture of sexes and ages in each. There didn't appear to be any specific order, apart from the fact they kept the healthier ones closer to the door.

Jane clung to my arm as we walked down the narrow path, peering inside each cage. Her people stood and approached the glass wall and watched us with large eyes. It broke my heart to see them in such a state, I could only image what Jane was going through.

As we reached the far end, Jane gasped. The smell of urine, rotting flesh, and blood was strongest here.

Jane dusted tears from her cheeks and neared the barrier. She pressed her right palm against the glass when one occupant saw her and neared. She too pressed her palm against the glass, tears welling in her eyes.

"Penne," Jane croaked. "What happened?"

"Get out of here, Jane. Before Rhett sees you," Penne whispered hoarsely. Her face gaunt, her eyes dark and sunken, and she must have lost quite a lot of weight. Her skin loose, leathery and thin on her frame. She'd also lost hair but still had gray patches growing in certain spots.

When I first saw Jane, her hair looked dull and her skin tone almost gray. What Rhett had done to her people was much worse. Penne's appearance was ghostly, bordering her grave.

"What did he do to you?"

"Things he'll do to you. Leave—"

"Not without my people," Jane said, glancing down the narrow corridor, then turned back to Penne. "Do you know where he is?"

Penne shook her head slowly. It looked painful to move. "He was here about twenty minutes ago." Penne cleared her throat. That too looked like it hurt. "He only comes here to take one of us or if anyone has died."

"Where does he take them?" Jane asked.

"He has a room below," — she pointed down, — "it's his private room. He only takes the females there. The others he takes to one of the medical rooms for extraction."

Christ, I wanted to inflict as much pain as I could on this guy. It sounded like Rhett was doing more than just taking their essence.

Jane white knuckled the cage handle.

"Should I try to open them?" I asked, carefully pushing Jane aside.

"Yes, I'll stand by the door and let you know if anyone comes."

I glanced up, grateful no cameras watched us or there would be an army after us. I doubted Rhett wanted evidence of his torture chambers and would rather have his prisoners checked personally.

I glimpsed the lock mechanism keeping Penne and the others inside, and it was a simple lock. It took two movements with my lock pick before the lock clicked and I pushed open the door. I did the same for the remaining cages and freed everyone. Now to get everyone out.

I exited the room first, ensuring none of the guards were around. As I entered the hallway, footsteps neared, followed by yelling.

I pushed Jane back inside the room and pressed my fingers to my lips. The others shushed each other and waited.

The footsteps became louder. I readied myself. Power thrummed at my fingertips, and I rounded my shoulders. I stretched my arms and stood in my fighting stance with my weapons raised.

As they ran up the stairs, Paul ran down the hallway towards us. He fired at someone in one room, then before the next person exited he shot at them too.

The guards stormed the hallway. They fired at Paul then when they realized I was in the room where they kept their hostages; they fired at me. We returned fire, taking them down one at a time, but more entered the hallway.

"Nice of you to get here," I said when Paul stood beside me like old times.

"You ready to blow this popsicle stand?"

"You know it!"

We advanced on the approaching bad guys. We used our knives, guns, and hands to stop them. One nicked my shoulder, another shot at Paul, missing his head by an inch. Paul retaliated and sliced his throat.

The carnage was gruesome. We had to use force, or we'd be the ones lying on the ground.

Those healthy enough joined us in the fight. I handed my knife to Josiah. He was my height, his hair sandy brown and eyes as blue as clear water. He nodded his approval as he gripped the handle and stabbed the man who lunged at him.

Paul offered his knife to a tall man with black hair and dark eyes. He rejected the knife and fought with his fists. Being stuck in a glass cage for weeks hadn't depleted his energy reserves as he struck his opponent with such force. I was sure I heard his neck snap. Then he crumpled to the ground.

"Remind me not to piss you off," I said to him. He grinned and advanced forward. I didn't blame him. I'd take my frustration out on the men who held me captive and treated my people worse than animals. It was appalling how we'd found them. I was just relieved we arrived when we did.

When we'd worked our way through the scumbags, we descended the stairs. We needed a large enough vehicle to transport everyone to safety, but first I needed to take care of Rhett.

"That's his office," Penne said, pointing her shaky finger at a dark area on the far side of the warehouse. Jane kept her upright, and I hoped she would recover. I didn't think Jane would take it well if she reunited with her sister just to watch her die.

"Get them out," I said to Paul, "and make sure no-one follows you. I'll use the ATV when I'm done."

"You aren't staying here by yourself," Jane said with concern.

"Honey, you need to get your people to safety. Go to my cabin while I sort out this man."

Jane hesitated. She seemed conflicted at the thought of leaving me.

"I'll be fine." I cupped her face and kissed her chastely. "Now go."

Reluctantly, Jane joined her people. She half carried her sister as they traversed down the hallway. She kept glancing over her shoulder at me, her expression filled with something akin to sadness or regret.

I turned and headed in the direction of Rhett's office.

Chapter Sixteen

BYRON

Even with the commotion of our fight upstairs, I found Rhett calmly sitting behind his desk. Waiting. It's like he knew we were coming for him and didn't bother attacking first or escaping. Unless…

Unless he had a backup plan and was biding his time, waiting for someone to help him escape or to kill us. A man with his means had an army or another compound like this one. I shuddered at the thought. If there was another location, I'd find out where and destroy it, too.

"I thought you'd be running with your tail between your legs," I said as I entered his office. Not wanting any surprises, I checked behind the door and curtain near the bed. I flinched at the blood-soaked tissue paper in the wastebasket. The bed reminded me of those in a gynecologist's office, where women placed their legs in stirrups.

I squeezed the hilt of the spare dagger in my right hand and the handle of my pistol in the other, and neared. I wanted to make him scream from the pain he deserved.

Rhett gave a sly grin. He obviously took gratification in seeing my discomfort at the sight of his room.

"You're sick."

"I did not poke them with my stick." He combed his fingers through his black hair. His dark eyes not once leaving me. "It was artificial insemination performed by one of my doctors. My room is the most comfortable. The light here is better, and besides, I'm saving myself for Jane." His arm moved under the desk and he winked.

Rage filled my veins at the thought of him touching Jane.

Recognition flashed in his dark gaze, and he smirked. "Are you in love with her? It's a pity," — he picked up his steel barrel pen and pocketed it, — "but she'll be mine by the end of the day."

I closed the distance, wanting to remove his head from his shoulders.

But he didn't budge. He glared daggers at me. "You've messed things up for me here. And I'm afraid there's no simple solution to what you've done. The men upstairs," — he pointed his index finger at the ceiling, — "aren't pleased with how this has played out."

I furrowed my brows. I'd mistakenly thought Rhett was the leader, but from what he'd alluded to, he was only the middleman. He followed orders.

"Who's your boss?" I pointed the sharp blade at him.

Rhett stood up with raised hands. "Someone you have angered, and he'll be coming for you next."

"Tell me!" I yelled.

"We know all about you, Byron," he said, changing the subject.

I narrowed my eyes at him.

"Are you sure I can't tempt you to work for me? I'll

make you my second in charge and all the money you ever dreamed of—"

"I don't want your money," I said through gritted teeth. The audacity. Did he really think I'd work for him? After everything he did to Jane and her people. He was more insane than I originally thought.

"Fine." Rhett dropped his hands and moved around the table. "I had to ask." He gave a gallant shrug. "You know, I wanted to give you one more chance before my boss comes after you."

I dared not take my eyes off him as I felt a slight thrumming power coming from him, making the hairs on my forearms and neck stand up. At my cabin I watched him swipe through the air like his fingers were knives and sliced his lackey's throat. I readied myself for any attack.

"Shannon is one of the most powerful people in Sterling Meadow. Once he has your name," — he pointed his index finger at me and I wanted to snap his bones, — "he'll crush your family." He fisted his hand and gritted his teeth.

"I'm tired of your games, Rhett. And whoever this Shannon is, I will see to it he gets what he deserves."

Rhett threw his head back and laughed. "Ah man, I can't wait." He sidestepped away from me and reached for something by the bed.

"Don't move." I pointed my pistol at him. A sound caught my attention near the door. I stood with my back against the wall, ensuring I had sight of Rhett and the door. If someone came crashing through, I'd be ready.

Rhett didn't stop moving. He lunged towards the bed, turned around, and swiped his hand in the air. I flinched at the pain, glanced down at the three deep gashes across my chest. When I glanced up, Rhett jumped through the now open window. I fired off a few rounds, hitting the windows.

Glass shattered everywhere, but Rhett made it out. I ignored the tingling feeling in my chest and dove out the window, landing knees first on the grass. I glanced up as Rhett ran towards the far end of the building. Whatever flavor evil he was, he was fast.

I stumbled to my feet and dashed after him. The wound in my chest prickled, but the sting didn't last. When a shudder ran through me, I pulled my shirt down to see the wounds knitting closed. The golden tattoo on my wrist glowed as the power Jane had shared with me took effect, healing me.

My muscles pumped as I ran harder. I caught up to Rhett and crashed onto his back. We both landed on the gravel, him eating dirt and stones.

I kneed his spine, keeping my leg there, gripped his oily black hair, and yanked his head back. Blood dripped down his face from the stones he'd kissed, and he moaned.

He lashed out at me, trying to grab my wrist, but I smashed my fist into his jaw before he could swipe the air again with his sharp fingers. The impact snapped his head to the side, and his body went limp. I pushed his head into the gravel until I felt the stones crunching into his face, then climbed off.

The sounds of blades slapping the air caught my attention, and I turned towards it. A large helicopter neared.

Rhett moaned as he pushed to his knees, wiping blood off his face. When he heard the helicopter approach, he laughed. "There's no way you'll ever get to Shannon. He has military men scarier than your worst nightmare. You're no match for them." He exhaled and spit blood to one side.

The transport helicopter was large enough to carry Rhett and all his men. I knew Paul could fly it and watched as he ran towards the helicopter as it landed. He probably thought the same thing. We could use it to airlift Jane's people.

Movement caught my eye. Rhett stood. He turned around and faced me. He didn't run again. I suspected he knew he couldn't get to the helicopter in time and that he'd met his match. It was time he faced his fate.

Rhett rounded his shoulders and shook out his arms. He brought his fists near his face and bounced on his toes, ready to fight.

I nodded my understanding and would provide the hand-to-hand combat. I dropped my weapon but sheathed the blade. I didn't trust this guy and would use it if he fought dirty.

I didn't wait for him to start the fight. I took two steps closer to him and smashed my fist into his cheek. He moaned and touched his cheek; the skin there had split and bled.

He aimed for my face, but I swatted his hand away and punched him in the nose. He doubled over as blood poured out his nose. When he stood straight, he wiped the blood with the back of his hand, wearing a scowl, but it didn't stop bleeding.

"I'm going to hurt you for that." He promised, and bounced on his toes. He performed a high kick while I tried to get out of his way. But he didn't see it through. Instead, he used misdirection and knew where I'd advance to and swiped his left fist at me, hitting me in the jaw.

I moaned and rubbed my aching face. Rhett grinned and advanced again. I wouldn't fall for his kick again, and as he approached, I kicked his side. He caught my ankle before I could strike, and he twisted my foot. I collapsed to the ground as pain shot up my leg. It felt as though he'd broken my ankle, but when I pushed away from him and moved my foot; the pain ebbed and receded. Luckily it didn't break or I just healed that quickly.

Rhett continued rocking on his feet.

I glanced in the helicopter's direction; the pilot unconscious on the ground with Paul helping everyone aboard.

Jane stood to one side, staring at me.

As I turned to face Rhett, he charged at me. He pushed his shoulder into my sternum and we both fell hard. He knocked the wind out of me and I struggled to breathe.

I wanted this to end. I'd played enough with this guy and pulled out my knife, thrusting it into his side and yanked down. He yelled, smashing his elbow into my face. I dropped the knife but scrambled to reach it again.

Rhett dove, grabbing the knife before I could get it. While he was on the ground, a light caught my attention and remembered the expensive steel barrel pen he pocketed. Within seconds I grabbed the pen, gripped it firmly in my hand and pushed the plunger, keeping my thumb there, and drove it into his neck, repeatedly stabbing him.

Rhett swung blindly, slicing my left forearm that protected my face. He collapsed onto his back, his free hand grabbing his neck as blood pumped out the fresh holes I'd made.

Rhett made gargling sounds as blood continued pulsing out his neck until it slowed and his breathing stopped. His arms collapsed to his sides as he stared glassy eyed at the gloomy sky above us, the sun hiding behind thick clouds.

I stood slowly, assessing my wounds. I felt stiff with bumps and bruises everywhere. The cuts on my forearm already started knitting together.

The sound of someone running caught my attention, and I glanced up to see Jane. Her face glistened with tears as she reached out for me. I embraced her, never wanting to let go.

"I thought he was going to kill you," she cried, wiping her eyes.

"It's alright. I think that boost of your power helped me." I kissed the top of her head. "Come." I gripped her hand. "Let's get out of here."

Chapter Seventeen

JANE

Paul flew the helicopter towards Sterling Meadow's medical facility. They gave the all clear for us to land on the roof, where medical staff awaited our arrival.

The hospital staff tended to everyone, and those who required additional treatment stayed overnight. They admitted my sister Penne into ICU for organ failure. Rhett had extracted so much of her essence, without killing her, that it left her on death's door. Because of the extraction, she couldn't heal herself.

The same happened to my brother, who was in the OR for spinal surgery. He'd been in the same cage as Penne, but unable to stand. We're hoping the surgery restored feeling to his legs.

Two pregnant women had asked for abortions. They did not want to carry Rhett's children and considered them abominations. Although Rhett raped no-one, they carried his children. The doctors agreed, only because they were about five weeks pregnant. Luckily, our kind didn't struggle to conceive, and the two women would try again once they found their mates.

Before we left the compound, Byron went back inside to destroy the buildings. He exited the bottom building with a bag over his shoulder, dragged Rhett's body back inside the building, and exited the buildings as they exploded into raging infernos.

The lab ignited along with all the vials containing my people's essence. Those expecting the vials would have to live without it. Byron was adamant on tracking down those responsible and killing them, too. He even informed his old boss about what had happened, and with Paul's confirmation, the military would intervene.

I snuggled into the curve of Byron's body as we waited to hear about everyone's condition. Paul had stayed with us after they stitched his back. Apparently someone used his body as a pincushion, but all the wounds were superficial.

Paul read a newspaper while we waited.

Byron kept kissing the top of my head or my temple. Like he needed a reminder I was by his side. I didn't mind, he could kiss me all day long.

I sighed with relief that everything worked out and although I'd lost some of my people, most had survived the ordeal. It would take time to recover, but they were free and Rhett destroyed.

Byron flinched and let go of me. He reached for Paul's newspaper, reading the front page. "It's him," he said, pointing at a picture of a man with long blond hair. The caption read, *'Shannon's evil deeds exposed. The man captured.'*

"Who's that?" I asked, watching Byron carefully.

"I can't believe it. This is the guy Rhett spoke about. It has to be." Byron read the article and nodded. "Yep, this is the guy. Apparently he experimented on supernaturals and extracted their DNA and did many illegal things. I guess they did our job for us now that they've taken care of the guy at the top." He smiled and pulled me into an embrace, exhaling loudly.

"At least we're safe now." I mumbled into his neck.

"Yes," Byron said, rubbing my back. "A leader from the Were-Animal Alliance is coming. He wants to reach out to you and offer his protection."

"Huh? When did this happen?" I asked, sitting back to look at Byron. It left me on edge knowing they were coming here to speak with me. What if they wanted to hurt us? My people couldn't endure another round of torture.

"Don't look so worried, Jane. It's good news, I promise." Byron brushed his knuckles lightly against my cheek. "While you were with your sister, a man approached upon hearing what had happened to your people. Apparently news travels fast in this small town."

"The were-animals look after each other in this town," Paul said, resting his elbows on his knees. "For their leader to seek you out is good for you and your people."

I exhaled a shaky breath, hoping this was true. I wondered how they came to hear about us. "Perhaps they have a doctor who spies on them here," I offered, glancing at the nurses at their station. "They knew what to do with us. It was comforting and scary that I didn't have to explain anything. It's as if they knew what we were." I admitted now that I thought about it. And they didn't give me the feeling that I should be weary of the medical staff.

"Maybe," Byron said, pulling me back to him. "Everyone is safe. If there's trouble again, you have the WAA," he said with a smile. "I on the other hand, will always be there to protect you."

"Yes, you will." I snuggled into him, his heat comforting.

An imposing man with broad shoulders and blond hair approached us with purpose. My hands started sweating, and I clung to Byron like a little monkey. When he neared, he smiled, his light brown eyes twinkling with humor, as if realizing he frightened me.

"Hi, I'm Troy, lion alpha and a leader with the WAA." He proffered his hand, and I took it to shake. His hand was warm and dry. "You must be Jane." His lips curled into a sincere smile that reached his eyes. The points of his teeth extended and his features shifted suddenly before flashing back to human; looking more lion than human in that split second.

"Yes," I croaked. Cleared my throat and stood up.

"Please sit." He motioned with his hand for me to sit again. Troy's honey-brown eyes were average looking but oddly captivating. "Now," he said, and sat beside me. "Tell me everything that's happened and we'll take it from there."

And that's what I did. Usually I was skeptical of people I'd just met. But there was something about Troy that made me want to tell him everything. He seemed genuine in helping us and attentive to what I had to say.

I told him everything that had happened to us. He admitted he'd never heard of hawk shifters before, but said the WAA would protect us and welcomed me into the fold by offering me a paying position as a leader. By working with them, I could learn their ways and become comfortable working with other shifters.

The entire conversation felt surreal. I had to pinch the top of my hand every couple of minutes to make sure I wasn't dreaming.

Byron sat beside me, his arm over my shoulders protectively. Even Paul remained seated while my conversation with Troy continued.

After an hour, Troy stood up to leave. He would see about accommodation for my people and would call us once confirmed. Neither Byron nor I had a phone, Paul gave him his number and Byron gave Troy his email address.

It was early nightfall before those who could leave the hospital did. A bus waited for everyone to transport them to their new accommodation.

Troy had performed a minor miracle and set everyone up in an old house large enough. The structure reminded me of those mansions rich folks lived in with their twenty staff members. The walls were in desperate need of a fresh coat of paint but otherwise it was perfect.

Paul rented a car and went to his wife. She didn't stop calling, making sure he was okay.

Byron stayed with me in a cramped bedroom with another couple. The room was small but cosy. The bedding warm and comfortable.

Troy hired a catering company to serve dinner, and they'd be there to serve us every meal for a week, or until we found permanent accommodation.

Byron suggested we rent a large house, like the one we were in, and make it our own. He even offered what money he had left as a down payment.

I comforted him by telling him my people had jewels and gold hidden underground and was sure we could manage something.

I sent one elder to our hidden treasure and to pay Troy for his kindness, and exchanged the rest for cash. Troy had mentioned a respectable jeweler who bought second hand items at a good price.

Troy informed us there were many jobs available for us and would pull more strings to get us enrolled in courses to help bridge the information gap. My people were keen to start their new lives, surrounded by humans and other shifters.

With our bellies full and my people safe, I snuggled up beside Byron and drifted off to a peaceful sleep.

Chapter Eighteen

JANE

Two Years Later

I sat in the hot spring and leaned back, resting my head on the outer edge, and glanced up at the blue sky. The yearly storm had passed, and spring was in the air. A butterfly fluttered past, sitting on a blade of grass before moving on.

"Mommy!" Screamed Lilly from the porch. Her smile broad and her eyes twinkled. Her sandy brown hair with golden highlights reminding me of my own hair which had grown.

She dashed down the stairs as quickly as her little wobbly legs could carry her and jumped into the hot spring. Hot water splashed everywhere, and I lifted my little bundle of goodness, bringing her close to my chest.

"You know you shouldn't do that. Soon you'll be too big to jump inside."

She pressed her head against my chest as her little arms snaked around my neck, her hands tapping my back. "It's okay, Mommy, I'm a big girl now."

"Yes, you are." I kissed her button nose and cuddled her. Advanced for her age, Lilly spoke more words than any eleven-month-old should and moved steadier, albeit a little wobbly.

She had already shifted into her hawk form without me having to train her. This happened a month ago and since then we enjoyed daily flights together at dawn.

It relieved me that I had no permanent damage from Rhett's actions. And when we found out I was pregnant, I told Byron I wanted as many children as he could handle. Right now we're trying for baby number two.

"There are my girls," Byron said, sauntering shirtless down the stairs. His tanned, honed body glistening in the sun. The golden tattoo snaked around his wrist sparkled brightly as the light caught it; revealing the two bands. He reminded me of an Egyptian Pharaoh. Now all he needed was thick eyeliner and thin linen pants.

"Are you chopping more wood?" I asked as he gripped the axe handle in his hand and grinned.

"I realized I don't have enough for our barbecue and I want enough for the bonfire tonight."

"I love the way you think." I winked as Lilly nestled into the crook of my neck.

"Hot, Mommy," she moaned.

I stood with her clinging to my body and climbed out.

Byron dropped the axe and approached. He pulled us into the curve of his body. We wet his naked chest and shorts, but he didn't mind.

I didn't need the healing qualities of the hot spring, but I enjoyed the effect it had on me. I'd sit inside every once in a while, usually late at night when Lilly was asleep, with Byron keeping me company. The two of us getting up to no good.

Tonight was a special occasion. Some of my family members were joining us for a barbecue, along with Paul and his family. We were celebrating the second anniversary of their release, along with good health and fortune.

With the gold and jewels we'd saved through the years, we'd bought a handful of homes near to each other for everyone to share. Some studied, found work and moved out on their own to start families. While others preferred staying close by. But there was always space for anyone.

We had lost a handful of members. They were too weak and died in hospital.

Penne had made a full recovery while my brother, Judas, remained paralyzed from the waist down. When Rhett had captured him, they kept breaking his legs and back. Judas was one of our most skilled fighters, and I surmised they thought he was a threat. He hadn't been able to heal himself after they extracted so much of his essence. And not even changing into his hawk helped and he couldn't fly. He even tried the hot spring, but it didn't work. The damage was too great. He would remain wheelchair bound until he died.

We readied ourselves for my family. Lilly played in her sandpit while I set the outside table with paper plates, serviettes, and plastic cutlery.

While I did this, Byron chopped wood. His toned body glistening in the sunlight. His hair and beard already too long and in desperate need of a cut. He wiped his brow and combed his fingers through his hair. I made a mental note to trim the ends. The thought brought a smile to my face as I remembered that evening two years ago when I cut his hair.

That night had changed my life forever; I found my mate, and he freed my people. I owed him everything.

The memories heated my core.

Byron glanced over his shoulder as if hearing my thoughts and smiled with a wicked wink.

Next in the Shifter Days, Vampire Nights, & Demons in between Series

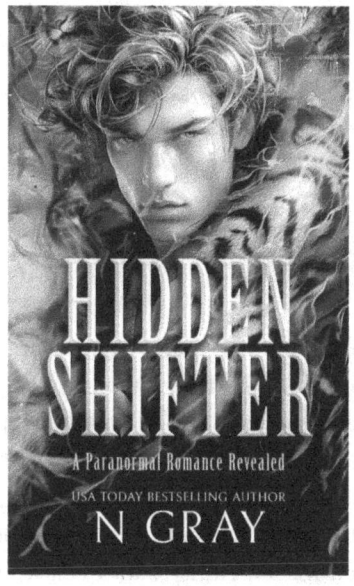

www.vinci-books.com/hidden

Forbidden fruit always tastes the sweetest

Hidden in an ancient forest, I found Tyler—heir to the last saber clan. Our dangerous passion defies centuries of tradition, but loving him means risking everything. When destiny and duty clash, can our forbidden bond survive?

Turn the page for a free preview…

Hidden Shifter: Chapter One

AVA

I couldn't explain it. This place was where I preferred to come and expel all the bad I'd gone through. I'd hike a trail at least once a week and hoped to catch an animal in its natural habitat. And, if the conditions were right, snap a picture of the beautiful creature. Then I'd watch the sunset; the sky painted in bright colors as the air cooled my warm skin, and the tension I'd clung to all week would dissolve.

Coming here was better than therapy, for me of course. I'd sit on the ground, surrounded by nature and absorbed the sounds, smells and everything my eyes saw.

Some thought I was antisocial, but I was selective of those I brought into my life.

I had to be.

I sucked in a deep breath of air, closed my eyes and allowed the cool breeze to caress my cheeks. My cellphone vibrated, snapping me out of my calm thoughts.

I hated cellphones, but it was a necessity in today's world; and only for emergencies. I had no social media and used my phone only to make work calls.

I glanced at the name displayed on the screen and unfortunately; I had to answer the call. "Hi," I said, trying not to sound irritated.

"Ava, where are you?" Derek asked. He was one of the nicest bosses I'd ever had, but painfully forgetful. I'd tell him I was grabbing lunch, and he'd phone asking for the writeup for the picture I'd sent through. Sometimes I had to leave sticky notes over his desk to remind him which story went with which picture.

"I'm hiking this weekend, remember. I want to take photos for next week's wildlife piece."

"Oh, yeah," Derek said, sounding lost in thought.

I heard him scratch his head. He had a nervous tick where he scratched the back of his head, leaving red welts on his skin, and sometimes his hair fell out. When he did this, he knew he'd forgotten something.

"It's an important piece. You know it's my dream to work for National Geographic. If I get the shots I need, I'm sending them my portfolio." I already had my degree in photography and journalism, and my portfolio was almost complete. I needed this weekend to get some of my best shots to package the portfolio for them. Ever since I was a little girl, I'd wanted to work for National Geographic. All it took was their show on the ocean to get me hooked for life. I wanted to do everything possible to help my chances. They received many applications on a monthly basis, which meant they only selected the best. And I had to be the best.

"Yes, yes, of course. It slipped my mind. I take it you're staying there the weekend?"

"Yes!" I said frustratingly; Derek paid my salary, and I needed to play nice if I wanted to stay in his employ. "You know I can't get the best shot in only a day. I need to stay here, blend in with nature and wait for the animal to come to me."

Silence filled the air, and I rolled my eyes. I shouldn't lose my temper with him. He was actually an amiable person; it was just… sometimes… I needed a break.

"What's wrong?" I asked delicately. It sounded like he was having another bad day and I shouldn't take my frustration out on him—he had enough of his own issues.

"Nothing, there's a dinner with my folks this evening and I was wondering if you wanted to join me. But if you're there, then that's your answer, I guess."

I knew he shrugged to accompany that loud sigh.

"Perhaps next time." I lied. I always said, 'next time'. Besides, he wasn't my type, he led an unhealthy lifestyle, and he was my boss.

"Okay." Silence filled the space again. "I'll see you Monday then."

"Yes, I'll see you first thing on Monday. Enjoy the dinner and your weekend." I hung up before he said anything else.

I switched off my cellphone and pocketed it. I pressed the fob, my car's alarm sounded and locked.

During the time I was speaking with Derek, three more cars had parked with the occupants going to the various trails they'd be hiking. Two people headed toward the one I was taking.

Once my backpack was on, I headed toward the start of the tough trail; I hadn't hiked it yet, and the ranger assured me the views were breathtaking and the best this time of year. It was also their busiest weekend and she was expecting at least two hundred hikers to come and go. The ranger had pointed out I'd be able to see most of the animals, which were scarce on the other trails.

I'd been coming to Sterling Meadow Forest for a few months and hadn't hiked the harder path because it took much longer and I'd have to spend the entire weekend completing it. The other paths were quick trails and completed in a day.

But I needed the trail where the animals were to get spectacular shots for my portfolio. I kept changing the photos in the portfolio because I didn't think they were good enough and I needed to finish it. My clock wasn't ticking, but I had to stop over analyzing my work, get it done, and send it off. And this weekend I had to get it sorted.

An animal cried, stopping me. I glanced over my shoulder and still saw my vehicle in the parking lot. The cries sounded again, reminding me of a wounded animal. I couldn't continue on my hike until I knew the animal was safe. If it was a predator, I hoped I could run faster.

Pushing through bushes, I came to a clearing where a deer fawn was sitting beside its mother's carcass. My heart broke staring at the poor baby, taking me to the first time I watched Bambi. There was no way I'd allow the fawn to remain on its own and dialed Ruth's number. She was a wildlife veterinarian I'd befriended when I needed to under-stand animal anatomy.

I didn't approach the fawn for fear of it running off, instead I waited in silence nearby for nearly forty minutes. When a loud noise sent birds flying, I stood slowly from my spot, keeping an eye on the fawn and sauntered to the path. The fawn didn't budge, but she watched me.

Ruth approached with her equipment and two assistants.

"Thanks for coming. I didn't want to leave her on her own," I said, closing the gap. "She looks to be a few days old and I suspect the mom died soon after giving birth." I didn't say I suspected something with large teeth had attacked the mother. When I'd first seen the fawn, I noted the mother had a bite on her neck but couldn't get closer for fear of scaring the baby away. Whichever predator did that had bitten the mother and left, which was incredibly cruel.

"Hi, Ava." Ruth handed her equipment to the girl on her left and hugged me. "You did the right thing calling me. I'll check her out to see if she's healthy, then hand her over to the sanctuary for rehabilitation."

"Thanks."

Ruth had shocking red hair and blue eye shadow. She wore a pink blouse, dark green pants, and green Crocs. Each wrist bound with leather bracelets and a crystal pendant hung around her neck. She was eccentric, easygoing and a loving veterinarian.

"Do you mind if I continue?" I pointed toward the path.

"Oh heavens, yes, of course. When you're done with your hike, you must come visit. I'd love to see your portfolio." She winked.

"Will do." We hugged, and I left them to do what they did best.

———

The winding path took me around one of the largest mountains in the area and the sights were breathtaking. I stopped near a spring and sat on a fallen log. The spring water was cool and drinkable. I splashed water on the back of my neck and wiped the sweat away with my bandana.

I glanced at my watch and I'd only been walking for two hours. The sun would set soon and I needed to find a place to set up camp before dark. I picked up my backpack and continued on my way.

It didn't take long for the sky to be painted in bright colors. Within twenty minutes the blues and blacks had taken over, bathing the path in dark shadows.

I stopped at an area not used in a while, but it would have to do. The ground was level enough for my tent, with sand and an old log for a fire. Since some animals came out at night, I decided against hiking in the dark, and I didn't want to spook them.

The ranger had mentioned the first main campsite, but it was much farther up the trail. By waiting for Ruth to arrive and tend to the fawn, I started on the path late. But I'd do it again. I couldn't leave the fawn on her own. Anyway, I hardly mingled with other hikers anyway, so the thought of camping out here alone was fine with me.

I removed my backpack and set up camp. The tent was up with a flick of my wrist; I unrolled the sleeping bag and placed it inside. I gathered enough firewood to make a decent fire for warmth and made some tea. For dinner I'd already prepared a chicken wrap at home, followed by a packet of chips.

I connected my cellphone to the portable charger and switched it on. Derek had left messages. He was sweet, but *no*. I vowed never to date my boss… again.

My previous boss/lover owned one of the larger wildlife magazines, and I was his star photographer—or he had made me believe that I was. I travelled the world getting the best pictures, but when his possessive streak worsened, I saw less of him. The result was fewer travels, but frequent visits to the ER. I knew I'd made a mistake getting involved with him; he was not a nice man. Instead of trying to go through the legal battles with the proof I had, it was easier for me to pack my bag. Naturally, he didn't approve and tried to *win* me back by stalking me. I'd gotten away one late evening, and he didn't have a clue where I was.

I found a small town, Krystal Creek, near Sterling Meadow, which I now called home. After a while he'd stopped calling me, and I didn't need to look over my shoulder everywhere I went. But I needed to know where he was and learned he started dating another girl, who was just as crazy as he was if the newspaper articles were to be believed. And exactly a year later I hadn't heard from him.

Once I'd arrived in Krystal Creek, I took a six-month sabbatical, then when I was ready to work again I found a job at the local newspaper/magazine in Krystal Creek. There were two reporters, myself, and Derek, who was the owner and Editor-in-Chief. Derek came from a long line of heirs to the oil industry, but he preferred to spend his inheritance on the Krystal Creek newspaper and seemed to manage the advertising just fine. I got paid per animal photograph, special features, or anything worthy of the space.

I read the text messages Derek had sent, and they were the usual ones; *'Let me know if you change your mind'*, *'I'll send my driver to fetch you'* and *'Wish you were here'*. He really wanted me with him, but I couldn't. I didn't have the heart to say *'No'*, but I wondered whether it was for the best. Then again, I might lose the only income I had if I told Derek I wasn't interested.

I sighed and deleted his texts. It was better to avoid. I would deal with it on Monday. Right now, I wanted to enjoy nature in all her splendor with only myself to keep me company, which I preferred. It wasn't as if I didn't want anyone in my life, I did, but the next guy would have to be worth it.

Hidden Shifter: Chapter Two

AVA

Splashing from waterfalls and swimming woke me, but it was only my aching bladder. I unzipped my tent, crawled out and grabbed tissues and a disposable bag.

I didn't want to go near my tent or the path. I ventured a short distance farther into the dense vegetation with the silver moon as my guide. Once I found a spot void of thorns and bushes, I squatted and relieved my bladder.

When done, I covered the wet spot with sand and packed the used tissue in the disposable bag I'd throw away when I reached a trashcan at the main campsite.

Glistening water caught my attention, and I turned in the direction of the rushing river. I'd never seen it so clear before. The other hiking trails seemed to miss the views of the river completely, and with the moon reflecting on the water, it was a sight to behold.

When I turned to retrace my steps, I couldn't figure out which way to go. I traversed through brushes on my left and when I didn't reach my tent; I backtracked. I ended up at the same spot I'd seen the river and walked straight up the mountain. Again, my tent was nowhere in sight. I turned around to get to the area near the river, but when I didn't find it, panic settled in. I closed my eyes and pinched my nose. I tried to steady my breathing and when that didn't work; I carried on walking. I'd never gotten so disorientated before that I'd lost my campsite. Next time I'd pack string to find my way back.

When bright light caught my attention, I exhaled thinking it was the fire at my campsite but then I remembered I'd killed the fire before I went to sleep. Someone else was here.

I carefully rounded a thorn bush, but my shirt hooked on it. I tugged, got free, but ripped the material.

Sounds caught my attention, and I neared.

Peering around a tree I saw a fire blazing, the red, orange and yellow flames hypnotizing. But that's not what caught my attention. I watched him lean on his elbows, kissed the woman's neck and thrusted inside her. His ass cheeks clenched as he moved above her. He kissed her gently yet passionately down the slopes of her breasts. She moaned and writhed beneath him.

Oh, my gods.

I felt my cheeks heat and crossed my legs. My jaw slackened as I stared at their sensual lovemaking.

It was not right to watch. I should feel guilty and a little dirty, but I didn't. There was something beautiful watching this couple—it was raw and sensual. She lay on a blanket, her long dark hair pooled beneath her, her arms clutching onto him as he drove himself into her; over and over. The man was tanned and much bigger than his partner. He had short, neat hair, with muscles in all the right places; they moved with such dexterity—like liquid metal.

My core tightened as I watched him. His rhythm quickened, she whimpered in pleasure and I watched with bated breath.

I couldn't look away; I didn't have the willpower to leave. I only regretted not having my camera with me—they were irresistible, their heavenly bodies entwined as they made love.

I bit my lip as my inner muscles clenched, seeking my release.

My hand slipped down the front of my shirt and into my shorts. I was so turned on it wouldn't take me long. It had been months since I'd had stimulation by my hand, and a year by another. It was by choice. If I ever dated again, it would be different. It had to be.

I leaned my shoulder against the tree to free my other hand and pinched an aching nipple.

I bit my lip again as the man grunted his satisfaction while she writhed and moaned, but he didn't stop—he brought her to the edge then slowed as he eased himself out of her then slipped back inside. He sucked on her nipple and I pinched mine. I wanted to feel his hot breath against my chilled skin, his teeth grazing my nipple, and I pinched the other one. I wanted his weight to crush my body, limiting my movement as he drove deeper.

The man quickened his thrusts, and I pushed a finger inside my wet slit as I imagined his large member pushed deep inside me.

Their grunting and moans were music to my ears as I neared the edge of my release.

When silence filled the air, my eyes focused on his deep blue gaze.

My veins filled with ice. My heart thundered in my chest.

He continued staring.

He'd seen me. He knew I'd been watching. He caught me with my hands in my pants.

Oh my gods. What have I done?

He sniffed the air and grinned. His dark gaze penetrated mine and I felt as naked as the woman beneath him.

"What's wrong?" asked the woman as she peered over his shoulder.

I had to get away. I had to find my tent, pack and leave.

I dashed from the tree before the woman saw me.

The forest was dark; the silver moon hid behind black clouds. A thorn bush pricked my face, causing me to cry out. I staggered away from the thorn bush and into a copse —one I'd never noticed before. Somehow I'd gotten turned around and was moving in a new direction. The faster I ran, the farther I went away from my camp, I was sure of it.

Leaves crushed behind me.

He was chasing me, and he was catching up.

The sounds of grunts and a low growl as he neared.

An animal?

I glanced over my shoulder at two glowing yellow eyes. I yelped and ran faster.

My ankle twisted and I collided with something hard. I saw darkness, something snapped behind me, and a weight-lessness seeped into my bones.

Grab your copy...
www.vinci-books.com/hidden

About the Author

A Multi-genre author writing twisted endings...

N Gray is a USA Today Bestselling Author who lives in Cape Town, South Africa, with her daughter and adopted cat named Miss Beans.

During the day, she's an analyst and provider profiler for a medical insurance company. At night, she types on her curved keyboard, creating fictional characters some may love and others you want to kill yourself.

She writes in four genres: urban fantasy, thriller, horror, and paranormal romance.

She now writes under Natalie Michaels for her new thrillers and SD Syns for her new horrors.

Acknowledgments

With special thanks to Rabea and Karin.

Thank you to my readers, old and new, for taking a chance on my books.

You are the reason I write the stories I do. As long as you keep reading, I'll keep writing.

I'm truly humbled by your support and encouragement.

I write in as many genres as I love reading in. There are so many stories swarming inside my head that I could never just choose one.

Horror is my guilty pleasure. I love writing short stories filled with dark humour and the occult, with a twist ending.

Urban fantasy and paranormal romance are where I love to spend my time, and I have so many books planned that I don't have enough time *(but I'll get there)*.

And lastly, my thrillers. Who doesn't love sitting on the edge of their seat while reading about what goes on inside the antagonist's mind? Well, I love writing about them.

Acknowledgements